EARWAX

Carolyn Balducci

What bothers my parents is that I'm going off. Parents are always a little funny in the head when it comes to girls. Especially fathers. My father when he looks at me, I'm sure he still sees me as a First Communicant. He tells me that was a period in my life of relative peace for everyone: I hadn't yet acquired the coordination to dial a telephone, nor had I heard of Women's Lib.

But Norm (short for Norma) Cantalupo is twenty and on her way to Europe lugging her camera equipment with her, for her trip is first prize in a film contest sponsored by NASA. They pay the expenses and Norm's job is to film Americans on the European scene. There's a commune on the outskirts of Amsterdam, some not very cooperative students in Paris, and some unappealing characters in Milan— it's one adventure after another wherever she lands. Corbett, an older, experienced, and interested man in Paris dominates the scene; but in her typically honest way, Norm copes.

In this second novel for young adults, Carolyn Balducci has created a wonderfully breezy, fast-paced, and witty picture of a young girl's experiences as she sees Europe for the first time, meeting some engaging and some not so engaging Europeans. She captures with a fresh eye the essence of wherever Norm goes. What happens to the film itself and how and why the making of it have left their mark on Norm makes a rare and amusing story.

EARWAX

CAROLYN BALDUCCI

EARWAX

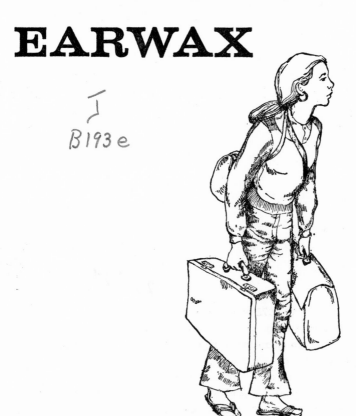

Houghton Mifflin Company Boston   1972

To my mother and father

EARWAX

ONE

IF IT WEREN'T for the fact that I had put down *Norm* like the kids call me instead of Norma, which is what my parents call me (except when Mama is really mad and she calls me Norma Maria), I probably wouldn't be sitting on this jet waiting for it to start and then take off and then land in Europe — which is to say Amsterdam because that's where I'm supposed to be going since I'm the first-prize winner in a film-making competition run by the National Association of Students of the Arts (N.A.S.A.). I mean, maybe I'm paranoid about male chauvinism but I'm kind of sure they never would have looked at a film called *Flower*, if my name, Norma Cantalupo, had been on the can. So I'm really thankful that the title was "*Flower* by Norm Cantalupo." I mean they would have thought it was just another dumb movie about flowers and the environment, that is to say Nature, by a girl who likes flowers and nature, which I don't especially.

I mean, don't misunderstand me — I'm for nature but I'm also for a lot of other things. Besides, I feel if you want something bad enough you have to pay the price and if it's a choice between 50,000 jobs and clean air I think the air might be a little dirty. Besides, there are a lot of things that people say and do because they think they've got to say and do them. Take for example music. I've never heard anyone say they don't like classical music. Never. Or take another example, shampoos. I mean, like my hair is long and blond. Now, you wouldn't expect that from my name, now would you? (That just shows how little you know.) So anyway, when I go to buy shampoo I've got to buy a lot because I use about a gallon of it a month, so I go to Alexander's or Korvettes and I buy their brand and you know what? Brand X, or whatever they call them, is always the same as the expensive stuff and they come in plastic bottles that won't break in the shower.

But what I was saying before is that people think they've got to go out and buy the junk that everybody else is buying and spread it all over their bodies and rub it into their hair because some glitzy model with a nose job whose age is maybe nineteen dressed up to look like a miraculous thirty is always staring out at them from two-page ads in those stupid women's magazines my mother's always buying. I mean like my best friend, Andrea, is a model and she's one of the chicks in those cosmetic ads. You know how old she is? Twenty. So what do Andrea and her age have to do with all of this? Well, it's just that you have to pay a price, you know. I mean, take Andrea. They pay her forty-five dollars an hour just for sitting around while they take photos of her but before they let her do this, they told her to go get her nose fixed and her teeth capped. I mean, like she looks terrific in the magazines, but she doesn't have a face anymore. She's too perfect-looking, like an old china doll in an antique store window, and everybody is afraid of her because she's so perfect-looking and nobody stops her in the street, hardly, and tells her that she's a good-looking chick, and even if they did, she's too busy now to stop and talk anyway and if she did stop and talk the pills she takes for her weight make her so jumpy she can hardly finish a sentence.

In fact, Andrea was in my movie, the one that won the prize, and she's decided she wants to be an actress. When I started the film she had a little time off because her dermatologist told her to quit work for a month so that her face could have a vacation from all that heavy make-up they make her wear even though their advertisements are for regular "natural" make-up. (Now do you see why I'm so down on this natural junk?) Anyway, the reason why I decided to shoot a film and enter it into the competition was because Andrea was available and yakking away about someday being in a movie and so I said if it was all right with her dermatologist we could make a little film in black and white so that she wouldn't have to put on much make-up. So the film started out to be a documentary on the flower industry. You know, the nurseries in Jersey, the hothouses out on Long Island, the flower market by the docks in Manhattan, the little subway dealers who grab your dollar for a dozen little rosebuds, and the really posh East Side snob places. And we got a few interviews with people who came in to buy flowers and we even met a few really nice guys and it was a lot of fun. Anyway, after it was all edited I showed it to some people and they said about the same thing that the judges said later: Andrea was fantastic. I mean, you know how sometimes you're doing something and it ends up that you don't know what you're doing? Well, this is what happened. I mean, *Andrea* was the flower. Like I know that sounds corny, but like here's this perfect-looking chick talking to all these people. Lots of things came across on the film. You know how it is.

Anyway, now it's June and I'm the big winner and Andrea is working and sweating it out in some photographer's loft modeling fur coats and stocking caps for some Christmas issue. And I'm on my way to Europe and the Middle East to do a documentary for N.A.S.A. on Americans on the European Scene. Part of the deal is that they're going to use the film on Public Broadcasting and in special programs around the country to promote European study-travel. Andrea says that it's going to help my getting started in films and everybody thinks it's a terrific deal.

They say they don't have as much money as they used to and so my project is to be rather low-budget and they were rather apologetic about it. But the assignment is an honor, they say, and they've given me a whole long list of good, cheap hotels and they've set up some system of one-man Welcome Wagons in all the cities I'm to stay in, though it's a very flexible schedule and all I have to do is telephone and there they'll be! Which is nice. I like moving about alone, but of course I won't be in New York where I pretty much know which streets to avoid. And, to be honest, even in New York I get lost.

All my expenses are covered, plus the prize from *Flower* will pay for next year's tuition, plus I may get a job after I graduate which is what I understand is a very difficult thing to do these days. Oh, and C.U.N.Y. will probably give me some credits toward my B.F.A. (in film, naturally) and, besides, I'd probably never get to see Europe — not for several years, anyway — otherwise, although as far as Europe's concerned, I'm not really sure it exists at all. The only thing I've ever heard about Europe is that it's a place to be *from:* people's grandparents are always *from* Poland or Ireland or Russia or Italy. I mean, nobody ever goes there to live. Most people go so that they can come back. I mean, like they have nothing else in their heads to talk about after they come back. For about six months local gossip or magazine articles or fashions aren't good enough for them and they've got to tell my mother all this stuff so that when my father comes home from the barber shop that he owns she can tell him all this and he can just sip his coffee and nod that old nod which means he's barely listening to her.

I mean, my family's Italian. My father's parents are from a small town in Sicily and my mother's are from Pisa. Now all I know about Pisa is what you know: there's a tower there and it leans. And what I've heard about Sicily is confusing because they're old stories told by my grandfather who left so long ago that nothing could possibly be the same. He left to avoid the draft, which I think is cool. I mean, in my own family there's an antiwar tradition. Anyway, my father is a barber. You might guess that he's not rich. Lucky for us, though, we don't live high on the hog. I mean, we don't need a lot of money. We have everything everybody else has: a TV, a car, radios, furniture, a vacation in the summer.

And my mother makes a lot of stuff for me. She's not bad, you know, and when Andrea comes over they go over a picture of a dress in, say, *Mademoiselle* or *Vogue* and then they go through the patterns and before long they come up with some material and then my mother sews it up. Andrea pays my mother for the things she makes for her; and so we're both always more or less on top of everything. So what if my father's a barber? I'm in college, and now I'm going to Europe. It doesn't bother me that I'm going and my father didn't pay the bill. In fact, I rather like that. I hate to see him spend a nickel on me that needn't be spent, because Richie's coming up now to eleventh grade and he has to go to college.

I mean, I know I'm good in school, but Richie! He's a regular whiz kid. Him and his logarithms and his tangents. My parents have in mind something like Yale or Johns Hopkins. But I don't know. I guess what's probably going to happen is the same as what happened to me: a New York State Regents Scholarship which gives me enough to commute but would never cover tuition at a college out of the city and, if you go out of state, there goes the scholarship. And for a lot of those scholarships you've got to be poor and my father earns too much, they say, for any of those inner-city subsidies which go to minority groups. Like I don't have any prejudices, not that I know of anyway, and it's nobody's fault that this is the way the money is being doled out, and I certainly don't care about myself because I'm almost through, but when my father starts yelling about "niggers" and "spics" (forgive me, but that's what he calls them) getting everything, I don't get as mad at him as I used to.

I'm glad I'm going to Europe. This would have been a bad summer anyway. No jobs. Me and Joe broke up last month, so that would have been out, too. Joe's one of those guys, you know, steady. Real possessive, not too much imagination. Though I've got to hand it to him. When we first started dating I was about fourteen. He's three years older. He was seventeen. Anyway, we used to go to the movies a lot. It started out with just any old movie. Just to be together, you know, and not having to say too much. You know how it is. Anyway, then we started going to foreign films: Fellini, Renoir, Buñuel, Bergman, Chabrol, de Sica, Visconti, et cetera. I think that's how it all started, this thing with me and films. So I should thank Joe.

What bothers my parents is that I'm going off. Parents are always a little funny in the head when it comes to girls. Especially fathers. My father when he looks at me, I'm sure he still sees me as a First Communicant. He tells me that that was a period in my life of relative peace for everyone: I hadn't yet acquired the coordination to dial a telephone, nor had I heard about Women's Lib. But the age of ten brought out a whole new Norma. By the time I was twelve, I had already transcended male chauvinism and had created my own reign of terror in and out of the family. They called me "Mussolina" and all the kids on the block would hide when my bicycle would come whirling around the corner with two baseball cards — one of Roger Maris and one of Mickey Mantle — taped to the back wheel. I was a Yankee fan. But they were winning too much so I converted to being a Mets fan until they started winning too much and so now I'm back to the Yankees, although I don't have the time to keep up on the batting averages anymore. One girl at school, Marie, was an expert at professional football but I think that was because she was on a different level sexually from me. I liked baseball because I wanted to be the first woman Yankee. Maybe I still do.

Anyway, in my family we didn't talk much about sex. It was there, but it just wasn't talked about. It's the same in lots of families. Andrea's too. So my parents are worried about me, alone in Europe. You know. And they kept trying to urge me to stay home and skip the prize. I think they thought I could take a cash equivalent, like they do in those giant sweepstakes my mother keeps entering because for every magazine subscription she has there are about ten separate mailing lists that she's on. Her favorite contest is for the dream house built on the location of your choice. She and her friends smoked crates of cigarettes and drank oceans of coffee trying to decide what kind of house would be a real dream house and where would they build it. Of course they never could decide on anything and so the cash equivalent was always their most plausible resolution.

But for *my* contest there is no cash equivalent. People who run student travel services are more interested in the publicity than in the contest itself. At least I think they are. And even if there had been a cash equivalent, I would have lied and told my parents that there wasn't and that I had to go over for school credits or something. Then they would have relaxed. If I told them I needed to go to the People's Republic of Outer Mongolia for credits, they'd let me, as long as it didn't cost them anything. But they still have to be concerned about my moral and physical well-being, right? Guilt. The foundations of parenthood. No matter what it was that I wanted to do, I had to meet with resistance, and the more they argued the more I wanted it and the more I fought. I didn't always win, but I felt obligated to present the other side. No matter what it was: staying out past midnight when I was fifteen, wearing mini skirts, getting my hair cut, or that time I got my ears pierced without telling them first, the dialogue was always the same:

"What kind of a girl would do a thing like that?"

"But Mama, all the other girls . . ."

"*They* are cretins and may do as they please. They don't know any better! *You* are my daughter and therefore . . ."

Am I boring you? Well, to make it all simple, let's just say that they wanted me to stay home and I wanted to go and, since you know I'm here on this plane now taxiing out to the runway, you know that this was not an easy thing. In a sense I feel I'm doing it for their sakes. Certainly for Richie. Maybe before he retires my father will take Mama and Richie to Italy at least for a visit. That might mean a large chunk of their savings blown, but they might do it. They were very interested in my itinerary and they even ripped out a page from an old atlas for me to draw my route on. Taped to the refrigerator door is a list of my stops and my mailing addresses. My itinerary was the topic of conversation for weeks at my mother's coffee get-togethers, all the ladies eager for details, nodding their heads with all the curlers still in and flicking their ashes into the saucers of my mother's second-best coffee cups.

My parents were not so much impressed by my

prize, but they were maybe a little hurt by my freedom, my cutting the cord, my saying: *You're my family and you have to stay behind. See you in two months.* They didn't like that. Not even Richie.

But everything went more or less O.K. tonight until we got to the airport. They were just starting to look proud of me, the prize-winner, when some jerky photographer insisted on posing us for some pictures. He kept saying, "Smile, smile." Of course we were all crying by that time but in photos crying comes out looking sort of like laughing, doesn't it?

TWO

RICHIE explained it to me once. The bit about how a plane takes off. Aerodynamics. I don't really believe in it. That's a terrible thing to be thinking just as this jet is revving up its engines. *There are a lot of things I want to do, God, so don't let this plane crash, O.K.?*

I am sitting next to the window over the wing. I am trying to think how I can climb over the seats in front of me if we crash and jump out the emergency exit that way or maybe I could break the window and walk out onto the wing. Nah, the glass is about an inch thick. Then this stewardess chick gets out in the aisle and goes through this dumb routine that I'll never be able to remember about the button overhead and how the gas mask will drop down in front of you for oxygen and that above you are the life preservers and you say to yourself, right, the plane is going to crash and I'm going to drop down out of the sky like a bowling ball and I'm going to actually have to mess with a life jacket? I look around while this little demonstration is going on. A few people are listening. A couple of little boys are really enjoying it, even. The guy next to me (out of the corner of my eye, the right one, I'm seeing this) is this really super-cool executive type. He's reading the *Wall Street Journal* and he doesn't give a damn. He hasn't even buckled his seat belt. (Mine is buckled.) About the only thing of him I can really see is his wrist which is relaxed and his paper which is folded up into quarters. My hands are shaking so I grip the arms of the seat. My knuckles are white. The engines are loud, even though we are standing still. They get very loud and we start to move. The jet is running down the track and my stomach is somewhere in Long Beach when the wheels lift up with a little bump. I calculate that if we were to crash parts of me might fall all over Babylon.

"You look like you need a drink," I hear the man next to me say.

"I don't drink," I say, turning somewhat but not letting go of the arms of the seat.

"A cognac would do you good." He is smiling a little and when I turn to look at him he's not bad-looking at all. A little beige around the cheekbones — the way that people who spend a lot of money skiing and going to Florida in the winter get around the beginning of

13

summer before they leave for their summer homes. But nice-looking for a guy who must be around thirty-eight, which is a lot older than anybody I know except my parents' friends. Or maybe a couple of teachers. "You look as though you might faint. And if you did that it would be a little awkward for me."

"I never faint," I say, wondering why my stomach feels so warm and fizzy.

The stewardess is taking orders. She's very perky in a Midwestern way. "Would you like a drink?" She is looking at him.

"A Scotch on the rocks — do you have J and B?"

"Yes, we do. And for the young lady?" She smiles so Macleanly that I want to puke. Maybe I'll puke anyway.

"Ah, she'll have a brandy — Courvoisier?"

"Yes." She gives the order to the steward. "That will be two dollars, sir."

"Here." I hold out my money between two limp fingers.

He takes it. I think I like this guy. He actually takes it without making a big fuss. Terrific. Maybe he's not so bad. He hands the stewardess our dollars. She blushes slightly. "Oh, I'm so sorry. I thought you were together." And then she retreats.

"No," I murmur, "I'm not together. Not at all."

"Are you sure you're not going to faint?" he asks.

"No." I sniff the brandy, not to be cool, you know, just to see if I'm going to be able to swallow the stuff. I take a taste.

"Slowly," he cautions. "You still don't look very well. Would you like a cigarette?"

"No, thank you. I don't smoke."

He gives me this funny look, you know, the way you'd look if on a payday your father says you can't have any money because he hasn't any on him?

"I mean, I don't smoke tobacco."

Then he smiles a kind of friendly smile. The *Wall Street Journal* falls on the floor. I take another sip of the cognac. "So what does your wife do for a living?" I ask obnoxiously. I mean, you know how sometimes you want to do something to some people to make them a little less self-assured? Well, this is one of those times. And you've got to know that even inside of my head there's this little film maker who keeps making me wonder about casting and camera angles. I mean, this little bastard in my head keeps messing with me at certain moments in my life, like the night I broke up with Joe. That's a long story, but during all the embarrassing silences I kept thinking, *Mike Nichols should be here.*

"My wife?" He takes a sip of his drink. "I'm not married. At the moment." Gives me another sly look, see, then takes another drink.

I must admit that I'm curious as to what he does. He must fly a lot if he can remain so incredibly cool. While I —

"Why didn't you ask if I'm divorced?" Eyes, Paul Newman blue; hair, Marcello Mastroianni brown; cheekbones square, Lorne Greenish; tender ears;

smooth, flat mouth a little taut over a crooked canine tooth on my side of his head, a gold cap on a molar.

"Does it make any difference?" We are above the clouds, now, looking down on them. The long June sun is golden and there is a weird futuristic sunset going on. The clouds form a fluffy trampoline below and you kind of expect to see some angels perched here and there. I look back at him. "Isn't that beautiful?"

"Yes, it is. This must be your first flight."

"Yeah."

"What's your name?"

"Norma."

"Rather old-fashioned, isn't it. Were you named after someone?"

"No." *Marilyn Monroe*, I want to say.

"Are you meeting people in Amsterdam?" He takes out a gold cigarette case and taps out a cigarette. "Do you mind if I smoke?"

"No. Go right ahead." I am curious about the P.C.M. monogram, the gold case, the *Wall Street Journal*, the pale eyes, hard as aggies, the hushed voice. There are creases under his eyes, lines at the nostrils. Then the old me snaps back into place like a pop-it bead. Out the window goes the Norma that reads *True Romances* and *Cosmopolitan* on the sly to land on the heads of harp-playing trampolinists below. "I'm traveling more or less alone."

"More or less?" he says. "I thought you were Dutch. You're not American, are you?"

See, like I know that there's something wrong cause

I'm from New York, right? And I don't have a Dutch accent. But at the same time this guy doesn't seem to be quite American, either. There's something foreign about him, so like maybe I should have suspected that from the way I talk he should have *known* that I'm a New Yorker. If he was really sharp he could have even picked out my neighborhood, at least that's what I read someplace once about regional accents. That they're very telling. "Yes, I'm American. I've got a lot of friends in different cities who're going to put me up." I'm not so sure I want to go through all that chickenshit about the contest and my assignment. "Are you going to Europe on business?"

"No. I live there. In Paris. I only come to the United States to visit my children. My son is thirteen and his mother says he needs me more than ever now. Don't see why that moron she married isn't enough of a father for him." He turns toward me. "How old are you?"

"Twenty." The cognac is very strong and very effective and things are getting a little faded in the borders.

"Ah, twenty. Well, if the argument ever comes up, I'm *not* old enough to be your father." He likes this bit and chuckles. (How did this conversation turn into "The Dating Game"?) "You know, I like you. You're the first American girl I've liked in a long long time. You're quiet, but you seem to be thinking a great deal more than you'll ever say. That interests me."

"Umm." I murmur, my head sinking back into yesterday.

"And I really detest flying because I usually end up sitting next to someone who is a complete bore and of course I'm always stuck for the six hours. Middle-aged executives in their moss green Robert Hall suits, divorcees desperate to latch onto me, giggly teen-agers, Baptist ministers' wives . . ."

The cognac is overpowering and much as I like what he's saying (it's nice being flirted with, isn't it?), it's impossible for me to stay awake for the events that most people dream of when they contemplate travel: jet-set romance and chicken à la king with little blister packs of mustard and salt and pepper and cream and sugar and butter and jelly and ice cream. (Besides I had my dinner at home with everybody there. All my mother's best recipes including lemon meringue pie.) About the last thing I remember hearing before the breakfast trays and washcloths are brought around is this guy's voice saying to someone, "No, I don't think we should wake her up. Sleep is more important. Lucky kid. I've never learned the art of sleeping on a jet."

THREE

It's VERY CONFUSING, going through customs, getting
money changed, figuring out where to get a bus. But
it's interesting in a jumbled kind of way. I envy people
like Corbett. That turns out to be his name. He intro-
duced himself after breakfast saying that now that
we've had breakfast together we ought to get to be
on more intimate terms. I suppose that I should be
shocked or turned off or something but in a weird way
I dig it. Besides, he's a Leo which means he's terrific
for me, being a Pisces. But after getting off the plane
and wandering around trying to get all my gear together we kind of separate. When I get out to the bus
stop Corbett is nearby, a taxi in hand, his suitcase
plunked on the back seat.

"Want to share a taxi?" he shouts.

"No, thank you," I shout in reply, the exhaust of the bus almost killing me. I wave the small, engraved card he gave me on the plane.

"Call me when you get to Paris!"

I nod. He gets into his cab, I board the bus.

I don't really know why I'm being so independent, but I'm curious about Holland. It's so flat and neat and pretty from the air. I want to see it from the high bus seat. The bus conductor helps me up the steep step and helps me buy the ticket. I sit down by the window. The doors clack shut, but we hesitate for a moment. Traffic, maybe. I glance out. A thin blond boy about seven or eight is with his parents. An older woman carrying some cloth bags approaches, her face a little flushed, her steps uncertain. The parents hang back a moment while the boy skips forward, smiling. He tilts his head to one side and says something. He makes a quick bow — a real dancing school bow — for the old lady and then thrusts a large bouquet of bright garden flowers at the old lady who takes first it and then him into her satcheled arms.

We pull out of the airport parking lot and turn out and across the gray highway into the city. I am holding two new things in my pockets: Corbett's card and the image of that little boy in short navy blue pants swamped by flowers and bags and his grandmother's love.

FOUR

I'M NOT so bad, am I? I mean, what would you do if you arrived in a hotel where you had a confirmed reservation and they claim never to have heard of you? I mean, what would anyone do? Fortunately it's still early in the day, and fortunately I've got no plans, but here I am in a city where I can't even make a faint guess at how to pronounce anything written down. (I tried calling several other hotels whose names I found in the phone book and I made a complete ass out of myself. This is after I tried calling all the ones that are listed in *Europe on Five Dollars a Day,* not thinking that every other American in Amsterdam is using the same list.) And I'm really tired from the flight, even though I did get some sleep, which Corbett tells me is very unusual. That's me all over, I guess.

So here I am, you know, with fifty pounds of equipment to haul around. And shit, there's no rooms here, and now that I'm here I want to go to sleep. So what I do is, I haul myself and my luggage out onto the steps of the hotel, sit down, put my head in my hands and start to cry. There's a lot of noise in the little street that I would be facing if my chin weren't down on chest. Across the way there's this canal and there are little houseboats tied up alongside the street. So I don't really know what's going on, and there I am, just sitting there, crying. I mean, how would you feel, your first hour in Europe and all you want to do is lie down and you can't because some idiot screwed up your reservation? Well, I suppose I shouldn't defend myself. Crying, you might say, is natural. Not for me, but for some other people, especially chicks. I only have to point out, though, that the end justified the means. See, like while I'm sitting there this little guy comes up the steps, *clomp clomp clomp*. He's got on wooden shoes. Would you believe it? Wooden shoes. Now, even I know that nobody *really* wears wooden shoes not unless they're selling Bon Ami or something and this little guy comes up the steps, like I said, and he taps me sharply on the shoulder (lucky for me he doesn't also have on wooden mittens!) and I look up and he says something which sounds like:

"Washingmachine growl?"

Naturally, my response is, "Huh?"

He points over toward the canal and I see that there's a woman waving at me from the deck of one of the houseboats. There are geraniums nodding at me, too. I wave back. She makes a thing in the air with her hand to tell me to come over to the boat. I look up at this little man in his dark blue work shirt and his navy cap with a little patent-leather peak, and I wonder if I should be dumb and leave five hundred dollars' worth of camera equipment here on the hotel steps or should I be smart and lug it all the way over there only to have her ask me what time it is in Dutch. I stand up. The guy grabs my gear.

"Hey," I shout, "put that back!"

I run after him as he crosses the street and goes over the little gangplank connecting the lady's houseboat with terra firma.

"Hey, don't drop any of that!" I shout louder than before, and I follow him on board.

He tips his cap at the lady, then at me. "Thank you." I stammer, wondering what's going on. He waves. Then he climbs onto a half-bicycle, half-wagon thing, the wagon part of which is filled with flowers, and pedals off down the street.

"You are a schtudint, no?" She waves her hands in the general direction of my jeans.

"Yes." Hoping that this was a good thing to be in Holland, I add, "I'm an American."

She sucks in a sharp little breath which sounds like "tuhhhh." "You need a place to stay?"

"Yes, you see that hotel over there is all full. I had a reservation but . . ."

"Tuhhhh, yes, they're all full. Yes, and at the end

of the summer when all you schtudints go home, it's even vorse!"

"Why's that?" I ask.

"Tuhhhh, because now everyone has money. The veather is good. But in August no one has money and and there are many crimes. Tuhhhh. Everyone's very poor then and the city is filled vith schtudints in the streets."

"Oh," I say, wondering if I really want to come back to Amsterdam in late July. I smile and nod. I decide she's O.K. "Do you know of any place where I could stay for three nights?"

"Tuhhhh. Until Saturday? Vhy you may stay here if you like." She smiles.

"Here? On your boat?" It's a little hard to believe.

"Tuhhhh, yes. Of course. I hate to see young people so unhappy as you."

"Hey, that would be terrific. I've never stayed on a barge before! How much do you usually charge?"

"Charge?"

"Guilders?" The word makes me think of a swashbuckling age of doubloons and guys in feathered caps swinging over ships' decks.

"Tuhhhh, why you may stay here as our guest. My husband and I have always made our little home available to schtudints such as yourself. It's our pleasure."

So I wash, take a long nap, have tea with my friend, whose name is Anna, and we talk about her relatives in Canada and the housing shortage and her husband's bookstore. When her husband comes home we have supper and afterward we go for a long walk around the city, which is incredible at night with all the lights reflecting on the water. Lots of young couples strolling, kissing, groups of kids just hanging out. We have a drink in a little bar — strong schnapps — and there is a lot of laughing and joking and when everybody hears us speaking English, the entire bar talks English and we sit there drinking and joking until midnight.

As I sit here in bed looking out the open window, the day seems very short and very long and foggy and clear. The window and the stars and the way the curtains puff out with the breeze make me glad that I'm here and not in New York and that the six-hour time difference is a huge *difference,* even though I didn't eat in any typically Dutch restaurant or see any diamonds or any Rembrandts. But I did have a lot of fun and I saw a man with wooden shoes on, which is something I can write on my postcards to Richie and my parents.

FIVE

I AM setting up the camera, taking meter readings, opening curtains. My contact in Amsterdam, Jon, is talking to the family. This is an American commune out in the Dutch countryside between Amsterdam and The Hague.

A child comes in eating a cookie. "What's that?" he asks, pointing.

"A camera." I don't much like kids.

"I know *that*, but what's that thing around your neck?" He takes another bite of his cookie.

"This one? This is a light meter."

He's chomping away. "What's the other thing?"

"It measures the sound. I forgot what you call it."

"An oscilloscope?"

"Ah, no. No, it just tells me if the sound equipment is working properly."

"What kind of tape are you using?"

"I don't know. It comes in a little red box." Jesus, I wish he would go away.

Another little boy, also eating a cookie enters. "Hi," says the first boy.

"Hi," the other kid says.

"Hi," I say, starting to shoot.

"Hey, are you taking our pictures?" the first one asks.

"Yeah!"

"Hey, cool." The second one grins and makes a terrible face and then starts running around the room and the first one follows him.

"Slow down!" I shout. They are barefoot and running all over the bare oak-plank floor. They are giggling and tearing around the room, which might have been called the living room except that there are no pieces of furniture. Just thick thick rugs hanging on the walls and a pile of them thrown against one wall. I like this. I think it is a good start on this documentary, two children playing and all.

"Astrid made the rugs," one of them says as he dashes past, almost knocking everything over.

"Careful, kids," a male voice warns, "don't ruin Norm's equipment."

The voice belongs to a thin young guy, about six feet tall with a nice fringe of red-brown hair all around his head and a brushlike beard. "I'm Jason."

"Hi."

"Jon told us about you. Very nice of you to come out here."

"Well, did Jon tell you about my documentary?"

"Yeah. It's a terrific idea. And he also told us about your other film. The one that won the prize. You into Zen?"

"Zen? No. Why?"

"I don't know. Something Jon said. Thought maybe you were." He smiles. His eyes are almost the same red-brown as his hair. "So, you're going to make a film."

"Yeah."

"Do you think you're going to do a lot on communes? There are a lot here in the northern countries, you know."

"Really? How long have you been here? You don't mind if I keep on shooting while you talk, do you?"

"Oh, no. That's what you're here for." He clears his throat. "We've been here since May tenth, nineteen seventy."

"Kent State?"

"Yes. We were all living in various communes at the time. Some of us were part of the movement. Jeremy and Lila were there — at Kent. The rest of us . . . just turned off. We met at Schiphol and decided to form a commune here."

"How come you left?"

"Well. There wasn't much point in staying, you know. America, Love It or Leave It . . . so we left."

"Will you ever go back?"

"Can't. The bridges are burned."

A new face appears in my viewer. This must be Alex Marshall, the patriarch of the commune, according to Jon's briefing. "So are the cities, man."

"Why don't you two sit down? You look kind of uncomfortable standing up," I suggest.

Jason and Alex sit down on the pile of rugs. The one on top is predominantly red. The two little boys come running back through the room with fresh cookies. They throw themselves on Alex, kicking and tickling him. He goes down. One of the kids asks, "Have you met Norm?"

"Yeah, she's neat," says the other. "She's got a camera and all that stuff."

"Are we going to be in a movie, huh?"

"This is Spock and this is Sunshine," Alex says.

The boys smile up at me, displaying cookie-filled teeth. Their hair would no longer be considered unconventionally long and their long, mirrored Pakistani shirts look more uncomfortable than they do unusual. And O.K., maybe their cookies are made from soybean meal; they're still cookies.

"Are there other children in the commune?" I ask, after Spock and Sunshine depart for more cookies.

"Yes, there's Vita's baby, Absinthe," Jason says, "and Kristel's baby is due in a month."

"Yeah. We're all looking forward to that, especially the boys. Could you come back and film it?"

"I, ah. Gee, I don't think . . . I mean, my plans

are a little too tight for a trip back to Holland before the end of July. But I'll come by and film the baby. Afterward . . ." A shiver runs down my spine.

"What are you going to do about schools?"

"Oh, the boys'll go to Dutch schools next fall."

"Have you tried teaching them Dutch?"

"Teach *them?*" says Alex. "They're teaching us."

Jason adds, "Norm, you probably think Alex is putting you on. 'Cause it sounds like what all parents say about their kids, but it's true."

Alex continues, "Yeah, we have Dutch lessons after dinner every evening. It's good for kids not to think that they're always the pupil and that we know everything. They're quick to pick it up from their playmates and then when they have to explain what they've learned, it sticks. Dutch is very hard to learn, I've found."

Jason says, "We have Dutch friends, like Jon here, but the last thing you want to do with people is to waste time having them teach you something. Besides, the kids love to do it!"

"Can I film you during your meal and lessons?"

"Of course. Everyone will be here then." Alex looks out the window. "I've got some things to do now out in the garden. Why not come out with me? You can see what we've done. All organic. I think the light's good enough. It's almost midsummer, you know."

We go outside. Under a tree a pregnant girl — Kristel — is shucking peas. A guy named Zane, a very handsome guy, shorter than me but really handsome, is picking off some bugs and putting them into a jar while he's weeding. The kids are outside. Vita comes out with Absinthe and nurses her while she sits and talks with Kristel. The boys set the table, a long wooden table covered with a cloth, and food is brought out by Lila, a strong plain girl with the squint and strength of a Bernadette Devlin. The dinner is simple, all vegetables, and the Dutch lesson is a lot of fun. Though it's not yet dark, we go inside and the kids disappear and we all have an après-dinner smoke. It's all very pleasant and I get some shots of everybody enjoying themselves while Lila tells me about the action at Kent, and then everybody crashes.

I mean, I think that's what happened. I don't think it was the joint — at least it never put out the lights before — maybe it was getting up at 5 o'clock after pub crawling the night before with Anna and her husband and all that schnapps, and this whole long day of filming and it even could have been the homemade wine. The woolly redness of the carpet is really about the best I can do when I try to think about last night.

Bed consists of sacks of pine needles tossed over wooden platforms, only I'm unaware of this until sometime in the early morning when I wake up, cold. I notice all my clothes in a heap in a dustless corner of the almost empty room. When I turn over I see the muslin curtains fluttering like sails. Zane, who is also naked, is asleep.

I poke him. "Good morning . . ."

"Good morning," he grumbles, turning over.

"Did we make love?"

"No." He breathes into the sheet, eyes still shut.

"Oh." Too bad, I am thinking to myself as I turn over, too bad.

SIX

AFTER A MAD DASH through and under and around and up Amsterdam's railway station, Jon and I make it to the train just a few seconds before it's to pull out. Running around isn't easy with all my gear which Jon stashes in the compartment behind the couch because the baggage compartment is already closed off. We are both frantically out of breath, shaking hands, kissing good-bye, when they start to slam shut the steel doors.

"See you in Tunis," Jon says, waving. The train pulls out and I find my seat.

The train builds up speed gradually and not long after we leave the station there are lots of small houses whooshing past along a flat, blurry conveyor belt of landscape. It is drizzling.

Jon is one of those guys, you know, that are too nice. He was very willing to drive me all over. I must say I met a lot of people and saw a lot of museums and houses and bars and things outside of Amsterdam that most tourists wouldn't see. And you know what's really weird? Those Dutch painters — Rembrandt, Rubens, van Gogh, Vermeer — you know how all their paintings are, well, a little dull in color. Not dull. What's the word I'm looking for? Limited, I guess. Their palettes are limited, you might say. Well, I used to think that was because of some tradition. But, like, their paintings really aren't contrived. I mean, there's not that much light in Holland, and all the buildings in Amsterdam are brick and everybody over the age of twenty-five seems to be wearing browns and navies and grays.

But Jon was very good. We went to a concert one night. Another night we went to see an old Jerry Lewis movie, but I couldn't understand what was going on because it was in English with Dutch subtitles and all the Dutch kids in the audience were laughing when the lines were being spoken and I couldn't read the subtitles and I couldn't catch much. Another night we took an evening cruise on the canals which must have been about as exciting to him as my taking the Circle Line tour around Manhattan, but he was very good about it, and he didn't seem to mind all the tourists who were crowding the boat, not even the lady with the rhinestone glasses and the fat husband who kept arguing about whether or not the flash pictures she wanted him to take of the lights over the canals would come out or whether he should save the film for tomorrow when they were going to the typical Dutch Village by the Sea.

I don't think Jon entirely figured out why I enjoyed the Aquarium so much. I mean, I don't think he understood about my being a Pisces and this thing I have about the water and fish and swimming. He's a perfect Gemini: pale, a little plump in the face and rather easygoing. I think he liked me. Aside from the obligatory passes which I put down, we got along very well.

Yes, I'm all set. This train is fantastic. If they had trains like this at home G.M. would be out of a lot of business, not to mention the airlines. It's clean and comfortable. I have a seat entirely to myself next to the window, facing front. Alternate seats face to the rear, and the aisles are wide. Across the aisle from me are two well-dressed ladies and opposite them is seated a slick young guy, slick the way only an American man can be slick. Sort of latter-day Elvis Presley. In a very loud voice he's telling these ladies all about himself. He's obviously a salesman for some company but here he's just selling himself. If only his voice weren't so loud. The ladies are squirming a bit and when the porter comes through ringing a little bell to announce lunch, the ladies go hastily down toward the dining car. For a moment I am paralyzed by the fear that this creep will start talking to me, but apparently he has an interest only in salesmanship and apparently I'm too young and poor to be of any interest to him.

He takes out a little black plastic comb and smooths down his hair, then puts the comb back into his breast pocket. He adjusts the gold pinky ring with the bright red stone and then rises and goes toward the dining car.

Isn't it awful? Here I am an American being so critical. I'm sure I offend a lot of people too. But I'm traveling alone and so it's easy for me to blend into the background. Still, I wonder if it wouldn't be better to be a traveling Swede or Russian. Much more interesting. Americans seem so vulnerable. "You are very naïve," Jon told me. I'm still not sure he meant me as me or me as an American. We were talking about politics, as usual. Still, I wish some Frenchman or Belgian would do something crass like argue with the conductor about his seat and how he doesn't need a reservation because he has a Eurailpass like the guy down the aisle. I mean, it's so ridiculous. There's nothing I can do, I guess.

I go to the dining car to kill some time and to fill my empty stomach with good things. I sit down at one of the few places left, because there's a Japanese guy — long black hair, beautiful leather T-shirt, if you can believe it, and jeans — sitting there looking confused. He's quite handsome with incredible cheekbones. (Andrea would be so jealous!) And he's looking at the menu and at a little black book and then back at the menu and then up at me. He has a kind of panicked look on his face that tells me that there is at least one guy who's worse off than I am.

"Do you speak English?" I ask.

He smiles. "Anglais, non." He glances at his little book. "Français, oui."

Well, I can't tell you exactly how we communicated because his French was screwy and my French was also bad, but we somehow communicated certain things, like he was going to study art at Paris and I got across that I was making films and that really turned him on and we had a kind of conversation about underground film making in Japan and it was really cool. And he is a terribly high-strung guy, nervous and intense like a tuning fork, and his hands reminded me of two giant spiders, always opening and closing as he groped for words. And we kept flipping open his little book and drawing little pictures in it. It was an exhausting conversation. It got to the point where I thought that I was going to have to take a nap just to have the strength to go on. Like a chess tournament or something. But it was fantastic.

SEVEN

Paris. Garlic in the subway. People with long pointy noses. A small boy in shorts carrying two long, thin, brown loaves of bread. Café au lait for breakfast at my pension. The proprietor looks like Robert Mitchum. Exactly. Next door is a small restaurant. Wine, oil, and garlic, tinks of glass, odors and sounds to make me hungry all day and all night. Coquilles Saint-Jacques. Ice. Trying to explain *ice*, if you can believe it, in sign language. The Louvre. Massive. Filled with the same stuff as my art history courses. Only in class we got a better look at the paintings. Little talking machines for the Americans, sparking off its Italian treasure, the Mona Lisa, which I had seen in the Metropolitan Museum a long time ago with a huge crowd of other people, all standing forever in a long line and being presented with a tense quick look at it. It was kind of like going up to Communion. I felt like genuflecting, as a matter of fact. To see it again is like seeing your reflection after a month or two of not looking in the mirror. It's more than a painting and I think that's what makes her so famous. I'd really like to know how she got here. Through what hands she passed.

Then I go along and walk and walk and walk and eventually I come to rooms filled with Napoleonic memorabilia. Some chart over in a dark corner tells how Bonaparte was born in Corsica, which was an Italian possession at that time, which would make him an Italian except for the fact that he joined the French army and then became a French citizen and then emperor and I should care if the French don't?

Trying to get to the Arc de Triomphe. Quelle problème. I stand there pointing at the Arc, pleading with the two dozen or so people I stop on the street for help. "Arc de Triomphe," I say. "Où est l'escalier?"

"Oui. Arc de Triomphe!" was the response of 50 per cent of the participants in this questionnaire. "Je ne parle pas anglais" was the answer of 29 per cent. Ten per cent gave no answer but walked quickly on. Nine per cent shouted "impérialiste!" and roughly 2 per cent said "Vive de Gaulle."

After walking in a complete circle around the Place de l'Etoile (you can't cross the street because the drivers are driving around and around forever and they don't like Americans either), I find a little tunnel, like a subway entrance, which leads under the street to the arch. I emerge for a marvelous view in all directions of Paris and Parisian carbon monoxide.

By the Tomb of the Unknown Soldier, I sit writing postcards.

Dear Mom and Dad,

Amsterdam was really great. I saw hundreds of Rembrandts. The whole city is filled with canals. Most people spoke English and were very helpful. Now I'm in Paris. Parisians are very chic and on the subway I thought I was in New York except that despite the Revolution, they will still have first- and second-class subway cars. First class isn't so great. Mom, you would love Paris. It's a very beautiful city. Nobody will speak English, but they do say things like "Bonjour," and other things I remember from high school. Miss you. Love, Norm

Dear Richie,

Paris is a fantastic city. The drivers are all insane and there are lots of kids walking around. French toilet paper is not to be believed: it's like wax paper. There are only three kinds of stores: food stores, lingerie shops, and shoe shops. To call long distance you have to go to the post office and make an appointment. After work everybody plays bocce. See you, Norm

Andrea,

Hi! Paris is absolutely incredible. You have to come here someday! Reasons: 1) the clothes are fantastic, 2) the food is fantastic, 3) the MEN are fantastic — there's one watching me right now as I'm writing this! He's sitting next to me! Turns me on! Hope he can't read this! Take care. Norm

"Vous êtes américaine?"

He's talking to me! What do I do? I can't speak much French! "Oui."

"Parlez-vous français?"

"Non. Un piu, er, peu. Un petit peu."

"Ahah. Je comprends. Aimez-vous Paris?"

"Oui. Bien. Très bien."

"Comment vous appelez-vous?"

"Je m'appelle Norm." Not bad. Just like the book!

"Norm? Je m'appelle Georges." He takes me by the hand. "Allons." He tugs me toward the underground tunnel. "Le Grand Boulevard — les Champs-Elysées." He gestures outwardly. We are in the middle of the block. "Là!" he shouts, taking me by the arm and dragging me across the street. It is like Moses and the Israelites crossing the Red Sea. They are all around us, cars that is. As they approach, they honk, the drivers leaning out and, as they swerve adroitly around us, shouting and shaking their fists.

"Là" turns out to be a small penny arcade squeezed in between two airline ticket offices. He stuffs the two of us into a tiny automated photo booth. He combs his hair with great care and pride, runs his long fingers down the front of his jacket, fondling the buttons which cinch the waist in, smooths down the impeccably ironed collar of his sheer cotton shirt which is carefully unbuttoned down to the hairline on his chest.

He's not looking at me at all. His arm is around my shoulders. He puts in a franc. The light flashes once. Quickly he turns his head toward me. His eyes are still looking at himself in the mirror. His brown eyes look like Hershey bars. The light flashes again. I am getting uncomfortable and hot. He's practically sitting on my lap. Suddenly he grabs me and kisses me. The light flashes again. The kiss lasts just a little too long to be spontaneous. You know what I mean. The light flashes again and then he smooths down his collar. The slim slip of film pokes itself obscenely out of the slot. He takes it in his fingers as carefully as he would a shard of glass. He smiles, inspecting only his side of the photos. I can tell because he has me covered with his finger tips.

"Let me see," I say, peeking over his elbow.

I look like a wreck, stray hairs sticking out all over, my nose looking like a light bulb. *He* looks like a movie star. In the third and fourth pictures, which were taken while he was kissing me, his eyes are looking straight into the camera.

We proceed down the Champs-Elysées. "Quelle sorte de labeur, ah, vous faites?" I stammer.

"Je suis mécanicien."

"Mechanic?"

"Oui." He points to the cars in the street. "Mais non comme ceux-ci. Les Grands Prix."

"Ah. Bien," I say, though I don't believe him.

"Vous êtes étudiante?"

"Oui. A New York City."

"New York? Habites-tu à New York?"

I was acutely aware of the transition. Partly because I was always very bad in French and I can only remember the obvious. With the impersonal *vous* you just stick on a word with an *ay* on the end. But everything else confuses me. His switching suddenly from *vous* to *tu* brings to mind *New Yorker* cartoons and Doris Day movies. "Oui," I say, thankful for the ensuing silence.

We walk a long way and enter the park and continue walking. His arm is around me. Both his arms are around me. He is kissing me with big wet kisses. Not unlike Joe, whose style in things like this was not so great. We sit down on a bench and continue. Maybe he's a garage mechanic but he'd sure make a great masseur. I'm not sure why I'm letting him do this. In public, yet, though public in Paris is much different from public on Jerome Avenue, to be sure.

Well, this is Paris, after all. Some philosophical lady with a little box and a bag walks by, tapping her cane sharply on the cement. She's not blind. Georges hands her a small coin, she gives him a small receipt. She nods. He nods. We resume. Children walk by. An old woman passes with her dog. Georges is persistent to the point that I want to laugh. I mean, people are walking by us. I can hardly breathe. I am also very hungry.

"Georges . . ." I say, pushing him away. "J'ai faim."

"Veux-tu coucher avec moi?"

"Un restaurant?"

"Non. Couche avec moi. Chez moi?"

"Non. Georges, j'ai faim."

"Couche avec moi?"

"Non." I pick up my purse.

"Tant pis. Au revoir." He shrugs, folding his arms and looking away.

I get up. "Ciao." I walk away and go up some stairs. He probably has some disease, I think. I turn to look back. He's still posed looking nonchalantly off into space. Jerk. He thinks I'm going to come back! Ha, jerk. Ciao, jerk.

I have no taste. Even in Paris. I pick the jerks.

On the subway, a little Arab dressed in a suit smiles at me and offers to take me home. *His* home. I decline, but at least he has a good sense of humor. I go to dinner in the good-smelling bistro next door to my pension. More coquilles Saint-Jacques and wine and veal and strawberries in cream.

EIGHT

I GO down the worn wooden stairs of the pension. It is about 8:30. I am ready for the day: two vitamin pills, camera equipment ready, a fresh pair of jeans on, and about fifteen dollars' worth of francs and more money to be held for me at American Express. And then I'm to meet someone who will take me over to the university where I'm to get some footage of a group of American students.

No one is at the front desk of the pension. "Hello!" I shout.

"Bon — jour!" sings out the concierge's wife from the tiny kitchen where she heats up the coffee and milk for her guests. As much as her husband looks like Robert Mitchum, she looks like what's her name. Fellini's wife. Giulietta . . . Giulietta Masina? The one

45

that was in *La Strada*. You know who I mean. Anyway, she is in a cheery mood. "Bonjour, Mademoiselle."

"Ah, bonjour, Madame."

"Il fait beau aujourd'hui, non?"

"Oui. Il est bien pour moi perchè, ah, parce que je fait le film ce matin." I hold up my camera.

"Ah, bien. Prenez-vous le petit déjeuner?"

I am amazed that we understand each other so well. I nod, and in an instant she reappears with a tray full of my breakfast: a thin mini loaf of bread, some butter and sweet jam, a pot of coffee and a pitcher of warm milk and a large cup. There's no one in the small room. I sit down at the one table by the window. There is a large bouquet of bright red and bright blue flowers on the table. I suppose I should know their names, but I'm not too familiar with their names, despite the film. There just aren't enough flowers in New York the way there are here and in Amsterdam. Fresh flowers seem to be extremely important, like good shoes. People look in the window. I feel a little stupid. Maybe you'd call it paranoid. I mean, so what if I'm dunking my buttered bread into this marvelous coffee and it's dripping all over my fingers and I'm a big mess. Does anyone else in this city care if people look at them? I think not. Still, rather than have to return the gazes of these people on their way to work, I look around for something to read but the only things in English I can find are a June 1969 *Playboy* and a ripped-up *Reader's Digest*. I don't like either one so I hunch over behind the flowers — ah, yes, they're called anemones (see I'm not a complete idiot) — and continue my slurping.

The American Express office nonsense is more complicated than I thought. When I get there, there is a long snake of Americans slithering out the door. There are guys with long hair and beards and knapsacks and a few girls with overalls and pigtails and sandals and then there are older people and there are younger people again, these well-dressed girls with pierced ears and long hair and short dresses. We're all here together.

After about half an hour I get my mail: two letters and a folded note. The note says: "I wait for you at the front. Michele," and the other two are: 1) a letter from Richie and 2) my one-hundred-dollar check from N.A.S.A.

> Dear Norm,
>
> Haven't heard from you yet. Creep. Just thought you'd like to know (because she won't tell you, of course) that Mom is going to have to have an eye operation tomorrow. She just found out and she doesn't want you to know because she thinks it might spoil something for you but I figured that if I were you I'd be pissed off if I got home and found out when it was all over. The doctor told Dad that the operation is simple and she'll see much better and won't get those headaches anymore. Mom is not uptight about it, so don't you be. I'll write to you c/o Milan to tell you the results.

I don't have a job yet, and don't think I'll be able to get one. So I may go down to the shop and watch Dad and maybe he'll let me do something. At least it's air-conditioned and there are people coming in all day. Saw Andrea the other day. She was with some photographer creep. Don't worry about Mom. See ya. Rich

I go over to the door. "Michele?"

"Yes . . . Norm?" She turns, looking extremely disappointed.

"Yes," I repeat awkwardly.

Her hands are in the pockets of her sweater. The fists push down stretching the cardigan. "I was looking for a man . . ." She removes a hand from her pocket and holds it out.

"I guess so," I say, extending mine to receive the firmest handshake I've ever had in my life. Quick, firm, direct. Somehow, though, it seems impersonal in its exactness. We nod. Her gaze is steady. She holds up some keys. "Shall we go?" Hostility, thy name is Michele.

Around the corner is a small, very small Renault. The trunk is filled to the brim with a tire and so most of my equipment ends up on the back seat and in my lap. We drive in silence. We go some of the way along the Seine. There must be other ways of cutting through Paris that would take less time. Or maybe it just seems to take long because Michele is not exactly the girl I'd pick to be seated next to in a small car. I don't exactly know why. Hostile vibrations, I guess. Anyway, looking out the window is a feast for me. I've always found humdrum things to be fascinating. But here, life is quite categorized: the dairy store with its cheeses, the vegetable store, the open market, the bread store, the wine shop; housewifery requires diplomacy, patience, and sturdy walking shoes. Here and there are splashes of sunlight and color. Municipal buildings display the French red-white-and-blue. And it's awfully hard to form the word *pig* in your mind when you see a gendarme, though I'm told they're mean little bastards when they have to be. However, it may be that tradition has the advantage over technocracy in that everything here evokes static, two-dimensional images. Maybe that's just to my foreign eye. I always used to think picturesque such an insipid word.

As if she had been thinking of something to say for twenty minutes, Michele now asks, "How do you like Paris?"

"Oh, very much. It's a very beautiful city."

"Mmmmm," she replies. I wonder if she heard her question and my answer at all. Perhaps this is a conversation programmed for natives who by some mistake end up in the same small car with a tourist. Then she asks, her dark eyes peering ahead at traffic, "Why do you Americans use the word *very* so much?" She downshifts and slows down, then parks.

I regret that I didn't take my time reading Richie's letter.

NINE

WE ASCEND a dark stairway of about five flights. You know how it is when you keep going and going and you're carrying a lot of stuff and you think that you're going to collapse if you don't stop but you don't want to stop, you want to get it over with as quickly as possible? Well, there goes Michele up the stairs. You'd think that maybe she'd offer to carry something. Not even a light meter. I'm stuck with all this equipment but at least I don't have to worry about her dropping anything.

When I arrive at the last landing, Michele is in the middle of combing her hair. I am perspiring and just a bit hungry and I don't want to put down the gear until I can put it inside the apartment. Michele is still combing her hair. I want to say something to hurry her up but the word *very* sticks in my throat and I decide that it won't do any good since she must be almost finished. After all, her hair is only about two inches long. But she keeps on combing her hair. I give the door two sharp kicks with my foot, though it's this chick I'd like to kick. She flashes me a nasty look as she scrambles to open her purse and put away her comb. Then she dusts off her shoulders imagined hairs and dandruff and adjusts her skirt.

The door opens. *Then* I see why Michele has been combing her hair all this time. There's this guy, see, no shirt, just belted jeans. Quel bod'. His hair is the same length as Michele's and just as carefully arranged. Behind him is a roomful of equally well-arranged young men sitting on the floor, leaning against the walls, and moving about. Some of them greet us — er, rather, Michele. Michele makes the rounds kissing and shaking hands. I'm not sure why I'm embarrassed. I think it's because nobody notices me. It's not the first time, but still, it's awkward to walk into a roomful of strange people (male) sweating and clumsy, arms filled with camera and tape recorder and stuff, and have to deposit everything like a maharajah's elephant in the center of the living room.

"Vous êtes tard . . ." Magnificent Bod' murmurs into Michele's ear.

That would account for the hostility. Technically the shooting goes well. The light is perfect, everyone does natural things like eating, moving around, getting up, and coming back to the group. No direction is needed. Though everyone is speaking English I detect one Irish accent and one accent that might be German. Everyone seems to have given me phony names. I don't know why I think that, but it's just apparent. Then they start slipping up, eventually, calling each other by the wrong names — I mean, their right names. But I don't say anything. They are rapping about establishmentarian educational systems and about how they should be destroyed. It's all very calm, though, as if someone were reading Thomas Paine. Who knows, maybe even the conversation is a big put-on. I don't want to stay anymore. It's not like the commune in Amsterdam.

I'm beginning to feel my fatigue, can hear myself wondering what Michele and Magnificent Bod' are doing, want to eat something. I turn off my equipment, stop the camera. Nobody notices. It keeps going, the discussion, and I go out to the kitchen. I peek into the refrigerator and find instead of food, boxes wrapped in brown paper. Odd. Out on the counter is a small chunk of cheese and an end of bread. This is it, I guess, lunch. (It comes to me that plates of sausages and cheese and a bottle of wine and a loaf or two of bread were being passed around while the discussion was going on. Typical Norm, caught up in looking at everything through the viewer.)

I wonder, as I munch my cheese, why I ever started making films. Without saying anything, I collect my gear, lug it downstairs, and walk until I find a cab. Nobody said good-bye.

TEN

SHE IS well dressed. Even I can tell that. We are standing next to one another in the Galeries Lafayette looking over some dresses on a rack. I am just tired, I guess. Tired from all that work and from traveling all around the city. I guess I just want to reward myself for my hard day. I keep coming back to one dress — simple, soft, and light. It's a dark gray knit with white linen cuffs on the short sleeves and a white linen collar around the wide square neckline. It almost looks like a school uniform with its silver buttons precisely sewn and its tidy, stitched seams. I hesitate. I should look at slacks, maybe, or sweaters. That would be more my style. But there's something about this dress. I look up. She is looking at the dress and then at me. She gives me a smile and a quick nod, as if to say if you don't buy it I will. I try it on. It looks super and it really fits well. It is in a paper bag, my francs are in the cash register, and I am about to pass the beauty salon when I finish figuring out how much that nod cost me: $73.

I pause. I look inside the salon, up at its art nouveau wallpaper and its high ceiling. Someone asks me something in French. I say, "Oui." I don't know why. Then I find myself being led over to a chair.

I don't mind. I think I'm about to get my hair washed and cut. It's really O.K. I've been thinking how dumb it is to have long hair when I never have the time to brush it properly anymore. And it's always falling over the lens and it's hot. On the other hand, I've no idea what exactly I want done. So here I am in this little swivel chair, obviously made for the pelvises of smaller ladies, and I am gesticulating wildly to the thin dark man darting about me with long pointy scissors in one hand and almost the entire length of my hair in the other. I try to push his fingers down below my shoulder blades. In a flash he cuts.

"No!" I protest.

He shrugs, as if he were maybe Chinese, and then he just keeps on, *snip snip snip*. Father Knows Best. It's all on the floor: a huge blond carpet. Tears sting my eyes. He takes a heated comb and some spray stuff and before I know it my hair is all in waves and small curls. I am a 1970s version of the 1930s girls who populate only the dreams of Italian film directors and Parisian hairdressers after they've had too much to eat. Actually it's not too bad.

ELEVEN

BACK IN THE PENSION, I take a nice long bath. Not too hot because I don't want to wreck the curls. I put on those soft suede wedgie sandals that I bought with Andrea a week before we left New York. ("It's like bringing coals to Newcastle, Andrea!" "But they're terrific . . . and comfortable. Buy them.") The dress, I discover, has two deep pockets hidden in the side seams. Which means I can leave my purse behind and just bring some money and my subway map and my street map. The thin wool of the dress feels good against my skin. I walk down the hill happy to be able to walk free of all that junk I'd been lugging around all morning.

"Ex-cuze-ay maw? Par-lay voos ing-lays?"

"I'm American," I reply, flattered that I'd been taken for a Parisian.

"Oh." A smile lights up her pretty face. "That's a relief!"

You've got to know by now that if I say a chick is pretty, she really is. This girl was a knockout. Fine black hair — black, not brown — green oval eyes, straight eyebrows, white teeth, long neck.

"Oh. Can you tell me how to get to the Left Bank?" Even her bright Banlon dress and her tacky shoes can't overpower her. Definitely Miss America material.

"Oh? I'm going there now. You have to take the métro."

"The subway? No. I don't like subways. Can't we share a cab? I mean, if you're going there anyway . . ."

"Subways are quicker and very cheap and they can't cheat you. Cabs are absurd. Come on."

We begin to walk along together. Men in cafés stare. I see some people come to the doorways of their shops and a few cars slow down and follow us for a way.

"I don't know about subways. I've never taken one. Won't we get lost?" I'm not sure whether or not she's as oblivious of all this attention as she seems.

"You've never taken a subway?"

"No. My cousin Bill went to New York once and he said he had an awful time. Got lost nearly twice a day!"

"Ah, well, I come from New York and I've found the Paris subway easier to get around on."

"You're from New York! Oh. My goodness, what's it like? All I saw was the airport when we stopped to change planes."

"Well, it's a little like Paris in some ways, though Paris is prettier. New York is much more active, I think, and it has more variety . . . It's hard to explain. They're alike in this way — what did you say your name is?"

"Cherri."

"Mine's Norma. Anyway. They're alike in that they're both unique. Paris is Paris. New York is New York."

"I don't think I understand. I come from a little town in Indiana. Green Springs — ever hear of it?"

"No."

"Well, no reason you should."

We are now passing a small park where about thirty men of different ages are playing boules (French bocce) but when they get a load of Cherri everything stops. A man in a sleeveless sweater over a white shirt and pleated trousers is bending over. He picks up the wooden ball from the ground and then takes off his checked cap. Cherri notices him and sort of glows at him and then she looks at her feet.

"Green Springs, eh," I say. "What do you do in Green Springs?"

"Well, nothing much. Now I'm at the university and I'm traveling with the glee club."

"Oh, I see. How long will you be abroad?"

"Gee, I don't know — three more days, I guess. We're only here for two weeks."

"Are you having fun?" I ask.

"Well." She pauses for a long time, her long lashes fluttering. "To tell you the truth, no. I — don't know what I'm doing or saying half the time. Of course part of that is being on tour like we are. But, I don't know, maybe there's something wrong with me but I feel so out of place. So foreign. All the other kids are having a lot of fun."

I think about what she's just said. "You know what, Cherri?"

"What, Norma?"

"I like you. Everybody I've ever talked to about Europe yaks away about the art and the food and the fantastic things they saw and bought. You're very honest."

"Well . . . do you think there's something wrong with me?"

"No. Not at all. Would you come back someday?"

"You mean not on a singing tour?" she asks. "Yes. Yes, I would. But I think I'd study French first and go to one country and live there for a long time."

"That's a great idea." I think I'd like to do that. How come I didn't think of it? "Where are you going for dinner tonight?"

"Well, I have a date with someone . . ."

"Oh. I was thinking maybe we could have supper together."

"Gee. I'd like that. But the situation tonight is very . . . you're not going to believe this . . ."

"What?"

"I met this man four days ago in Brussels. And. And I think I'm going to marry him. I don't know, it's just a feeling. I mean, he hasn't asked me or anything."

"Is he Belgian?"

"Yes."

"What's the deal about marrying him?"

"I can't explain it to you. I think even if he weren't handsome and kind and sophisticated I — I would do it." She adds slowly and thoughtfully, "You've never lived in Green Springs . . ."

When we get onto the subway, we don't speak because there's too much noise. Cherri is looking out into space, dreaming about her fiancé-to-be, no doubt. Everyone is looking at her, everyone. I mean, she looks American, quite definitely. She should have a huge purse slung over her shoulder filled with her passport and money and address book and an extra pair of soft shoes. She should shun Europeans and date some American guy on her tour and blush when he takes her to a strip joint in Pigalle and worry about lurking rapists and murderers and stare at the Mona Lisa for an hour and eat hamburgers at le Drugstore. But she isn't like that. I envy her. I envy her ignorance. Or maybe she just doesn't care. Or maybe she thinks everyone looks as beautiful as she does.

I take out my map, trying to figure out where I'm

going and I find Corbett's card inside. I nudge Cherri when the train stops. "See up there?" I point up at a simple diagram of the subway route. It's like the one they have on the F Train in New York. "Get off at the *third* stop after this one." She nods her head vigorously. "I'm getting off." She waves and I poke my way through the crowd.

When I get out onto the platform I start walking out the gate and up the stairs to the street which requires a little winding around. There are marvelous sexy ads on the walls of the tunnels. There's a woman playing a violin. I wish I had on an old trench coat. I would pull languidly on a cigarette and exhale through my teeth. Red lipstick, red nails. But of course I don't smoke. Cigarettes, that is.

TWELVE

Four or five people, so well dressed that they probably aren't Americans, slip from behind marble posts and potted palms and move liquidly through the lobby.

"Is Mr. Mason staying here?"

"What is his first name, please?"

"Paul Corbett Mason," I say, reading off the name on the card. "Do you know if he's in his room?"

"Ah, I'm not sure if Monsieur is in his suite or not. Shall I call to ask if he would like to have you come up?" He smiles.

"Well, ah, no. I mean, I'd much rather call him."

"Perhaps it would be better if *I* call. He may not wish to be disturbed." He smiles again.

There is something weird about this guy smiling all

the time like a rodent of some kind. I write down my name. "I'm going to sit in your bar. Let me know what he says, O.K.?"

He nods and smiles again.

The Ritz is beautiful in an obsolete way. Lots of marble. And ferns. Diamonds in display cases and flushed out onto the restrained wrists and throats of the few ladies floating about. Actually it's like a movie set very early in the morning, around 6:30 when some people have arrived — the extras and the crew — but the real stars of the cast are still in make-up or having their costumes zipped up. There is even that shadowy brightness coming from the skylight which resembles the aimless illumination of natural light impatient to be relieved by kliegs. There could be no restlessness on this stage. No scratching the head. No gestures. No perspired brows. As if the ghost of Henry James were the bartender.

Seated as demurely as I know how, I hear the desk clerk approaching. Without coming to a full stop he whispers, "Monsieur Mason will be down momentarily." He is gone in a flash.

Then Corbett arrives buttoning his jacket as he steps out of the elevator and into my peripheral vision. Definitely not an extra. Obviously the star. I find myself standing up. (Parochial school does this to you, you know. But his arrival in the bar is, you must admit, much like Monsignor McGuire bursting in on us in the middle of Sister Mary Michael's social studies class.)

"Ah, so it is you," his smile confident from sea to shining sea. "How nice to see you, Norma."

"You remember me? I thought maybe you wouldn't."

"Of course. Please, let's sit down. This is a good table. Garçon!" It's called *instant waiter*. "A martini for me . . . what would you like, Norma?"

"I — "

"Oh, yes, that's right. She doesn't drink," he muses to himself. "Sure?"

"Well, maybe . . . wine?"

"Un Dubonnet on the rocks, s'il vous plaît."

"What's that?" I ask, feeling dumb.

"It's a strong sweet wine. You liked the Courvoisier, you'll like this too. Trust me." He says this gently, though after what happened with the brandy, perhaps I should just stick to Coke.

After a long awkward pause during which I was asking myself what I am doing here, he says, "Well, what can I do for you?" He asks this in the tone of a man unaccustomed to being asked anything but favors. The waiter arrives with our drinks.

"You gave me your card and said to call you if I got to Paris. Here I am." I raise my glass to him.

He smiles, sips his drink, and smiles again, looking directly at me all the time. "So you are. You know, you must have a great deal of ESP." He takes another sip. "Cheers. I'm rather glad that you did come." He is studying me, trying to psych me out. He's trying to figure out what kind of girl I am. "Because not five minutes before I heard you were here, I had a call from a gentleman canceling our dinner appointment. Business. Generally I'm forced to keep the appointments my secretary makes for me." He finishes his drink.

"Not much fun, is it?" I say, already down to the ice.

"No, as a matter of fact, it's not."

More bejeweled women come floating into the bar. "Corbett . . . could we go for a walk?"

"A walk? In the park? Of course!"

The guy at the desk is smiling his ratty little smile as we go out the door of the hotel.

We are going along the street. Corbett has taken my hand, for some strange reason. We are passing the salon of a well-known designer. "His clothes would look marvelous on you," Corbett whispers. We stop a minute. "You look confused. What's wrong? I thought every girl wanted a beautiful Paris gown."

"And where would I wear it? Where does anyone wear something that expensive? Clothes are clothes."

"I like this dress. Is it new?"

"Yes. Do you really like it?"

"Yes. And you got your hair cut. Well, I suppose it will grow back."

"You don't like it?"

"Well, yes, I like it, but I also prefer long hair. My second wife wouldn't let her hair grow. I think that's one reason I divorced her." He glances at me. "Don't laugh, it's true. The bitch kept doing these things to spite me. She wouldn't grow her hair, she wouldn't let me buy her decent clothes, she kept cooking hamburgers. And every time she had a baby it was a girl."

I have to laugh out loud this time. "No, it's true," he says, grabbing me around the shoulder and hugging me tight and laughing.

"But, Corbett, what about your son? I thought you had a thirteen-year-old son?"

"Yes. With my first wife I did have a son, but she didn't understand my need to stay in Paris. She couldn't take the way of life I imposed on her."

"She's American?"

"Yes. The other one's Hungarian. Bit of a gypsy, you know." His eyes twinkle, though, as if he still admired her. "What have you been doing?"

I tell him about the film, about the people I met in Paris, about the contest, about school, about my prize. He seems to absorb every detail. In fact his mind seems to be opening and shutting file cabinets, storing my sentences under different categories and cross-referencing every word. There's something so meticulous, so intelligent and yet at the same time insane about this man. It's a cliché, about the moth and the flame, but it's true. Some little light goes off in my brain on some lower level, *caution,* but I dig it. I really do.

"Isn't it too much for you to do, all that carrying and toting?"

"No. I'm a peasant at heart."

"You too!" He looks at me sharply. "Have you read Adelle Davis?"

"Are you into her, too?" I exclaim.

"Into her? I *am* her. I grew up on a farm in Southern California." I'm impressed; he tells me this as if I'm the only living soul who knows and that I'm to be sworn to secrecy, even though I know that's crazy. "Everything we ate then was fresh. Absolutely no preservatives, no DDT, no chemical fertilizer. My mother baked her own bread, her own pies. My father would keep some livestock for our own use. We always had fresh fertilized eggs. That's why I love France. I have a house in the country where you can get all these things. Of course they're not cheap, but it reminds me of home."

"That's funny. The bit about reminding you of home. We're so far away from the States." And far away from my mother, I want to add, when she may be going blind.

"From *your* America, yes. From the city and certain *things,* yes. But not from *my* America. It doesn't exist there anymore. Which is why I'm here."

It is quiet and the pale pinks and mauves of the sinking sun cast a glow on us and on the spot in the park where we've been strolling. We sit down by a small oval fountain. A tall boy is leaning over the pool, setting his small sailboat to fly across the water. There is a round old man who comes by and sits down on one of the faded green wooden seats. He is fat and brown and he is smoking a reedy pipe. He taps his cane in time with some long-ago march echoing under his beret.

One of the ladies who takes your money for using the park chairs comes by. Corbett pays for our chairs;

the old man pays for his chair. The boy's mother sits down and pays for hers. Then the old man starts to talk to the chair lady. He nods merrily at her as if they were at one time caught in bed together by his wife. She nods at us and something is said about the weather and the beautiful sunset and that tomorrow it would be warm again. And how a little rain would make the dust settle down and the city much more comfortable. A group of men sit down opposite us. They are young, all in fine suits. The chair lady goes over to them. They tease her and she scolds them affectionately and the old man tells her to cool it. She gets her money and returns to her seat by her friend.

The sky goes from pink to Dubonnet to red to violet to dark blue then to silver. We start walking back.

THIRTEEN

We're in his Mercedes, cruising through Paris. There's not too much traffic but it's still a little wild. There's a large bus ahead of us.

"Corbett . . ."

"Look! Up there in the back of the bus."

I look up. There's a girl surrounded by clothes and furs and feathers and she's in her slip leaning back brushing her hair. "Is she a model?"

"Yes. They're probably off to a dinner show. It's almost time for the fall collections, I guess. Seems early. Well, who knows . . . What were you going to ask me?"

"I don't remember . . ."

"Then it was a lie. That's what my mother always said." Corbett squints a little and turns to me. We're stopped in traffic. Probably a light up ahead. "How come you remind me of my mother? You look a little like her, but . . ."

On the same subway level as that caution sign, a little blue neon one lights up reading *bullshit*.

"Yes. You're direct. Like the way you laugh, with your eyes and your hands. Open. Most women, even the ones who aren't as beautiful as you — "

I laugh.

"You are beautiful, you know."

"Young, maybe, you mean."

"That's part of it. I admit I seem to need to be with younger and younger girls the older I get. But the way you laugh, even the way you wear clothes. Very much yourself. These others, always trying to be something they're not. Coy, virginal, covering up their mouths when they laugh, dressing the way their dressmakers tell them. Look at you. In jeans you looked great, in this dress . . . something different. I've seen you sleeping, which is also very revealing." He reaches out and touches my hair. There's a honk from the rear. We start to move again.

"Where are we going, by the way?"

"I don't know. I thought if I'd drive around a while I'd think of a place, but so far all the places I know don't seem to be right. Too many people I know will come over and talk and want to inspect you and they won't leave us in peace."

"Are we near la Fourche?"

"Yes. Why? Do you know of a place?"

There is a slow ache in my spine which has now made itself known to me. "Yes, it's very good."

"Are you sure? It's not one of those damned places in that *Europe on Five Dollars a Day*, is it?"

"No, I'm sure it's not. I've eaten there two nights in a row. You'll like it. It's a neighborhood restaurant."

"Splendid!"

Corbett drives his sleek, silver Mercedes like a Frenchman, which is to say he aims it. I lean back in the leather seat and look out at the sky and the people walking in the streets. I suppose the reason I'm so relaxed is that the car is large and sturdy and the competition is just a bunch of flimsy little Citröens and Renaults.

"Now where?" he interrupts my headache.

"Left here, up the left side of the fork." We are on the right and then suddenly we are on the left, like those driving games at Playland where you stay in one place and the little road on the screen moves all over and you're scored on how well you keep the little car on the road.

We arrive. There are a few people at some small tables. There are several men at the bar and a few women. It has the atmosphere of a good restaurant that has the sense not to have too many patrons at the same time. Corbett sits down, facing me, sort of in a little corner. The waiter comes over and greets me with a note of recognition in his voice.

"I recommend the coquilles," I whisper to Corbett. I leave the menu folded on the table and look across at the bar. I catch a glimpse of heads turning in our direction and then turning back again. I'm a little fuzzy and maybe something was going on behind me that I can't see. Or maybe they're looking at Corbett. Or me? That hardly seems possible especially after this morning with all those creeps hardly saying hello to me. Corbett and the waiter carry on in rapidly boiling French. Maybe it's my hair. I mean, maybe the reason they're turning around, still, is that they noticed my hair is different.

"How did you find this place?"

"Oh, I was just walking by it one night." I have in the back of my mind something about not telling Corbett where I'm staying. It's that caution sign, maybe. Then again, he certainly won't just drop me off in the middle of Paris. This is the moment to say something and it's slipping by. If I don't say anything now it's going to seem odd later on . . . But with the way I feel in my head and my back I'm definitely not in the mood for anything but a handshake and a hot bath.

"No, you didn't. There's nothing here for you to see or do, nothing to film. Someone took you here. He's Parisian."

"Ah, yes . . . he . . ."

"Oh." He looks down at the coquilles which the waiter has placed in front of us. Picking up his fork, he says, "Did he break his date with you tonight? Is that why you came to see me?"

"No, Corbett. He's a jerk and I didn't want to go out with him tonight. I wanted to see you."

He smiles brightly. "Did you break a date with him to see me?"

"Yes," I say, devouring my food, enjoying the lie.

"Oh, good." Corbett grins.

Corbett, for a man who didn't know I existed two weeks ago and for someone who was supposed to go out with another guy tonight is acting peculiarly like a jealous boy friend. Like Joe used to, which was one of the things I couldn't stand. Not the jealousy, but the possessiveness. I mean, jealousy is O.K. when things are going well and when you don't want to go out with anyone else, but then it gets to grate on you, the way you're not expected to be nice to any other guy, even though there's no commitment on anybody's part. Men are funny that way. The possession thing they have about women, when it's really the other way around. If you think about it.

"Corbett, would you be in my movie?"

He puts down his fork and lifts his wine glass. "No. Absolutely not." I am surprised. It is the rebuff of a father refusing to play a child's game.

The main dish arrives. "Coq au vin," Corbett says. "Chicken in wine. How dee-vine. Gertrude Stein would say it's fine. Not to mention Alice B. Toklas."

"It looks very pretty, doesn't it? These colors," I say, gazing at the steamed green beans, and some yellowish dumplings which turn out to be stuffed with spinach and meat, and the brown pieces of chicken surrounded by a nice red-brown sauce.

"You should make a movie out of it."

"Like Andy Warhol?"

We continue talking, but the food and the wine and my foggy head combine and I feel like there's cotton in my ears and about twenty feet between my eyes and my hands. Through this cloud Corbett is telling me about his house in the country. I can't quite keep the threads of the conversation together anymore.

"It's high up on a mountainside. There's always a cool breeze and the nights are chilly. Everything rustic. White walls, wooden beams. I keep all of my books there. I go there on the weekends. To *breathe*. Would you like to go with me this weekend?"

"That would be nice," I say, answering some other question that someone else may have asked me in a dream. "Yes."

"Wonderful. It will be so wonderful to have you there with me. I like to be alone. But I can tell you do, too. The house is large and it won't be like staying together in my apartment. There's a lake. It's cold but we could go swimming. Don't bring a bathing suit. No one's there to see us. And there are fields and fields of wildflowers where you can walk." He puts a piece of chicken in his mouth. "The children always love it there."

As I sip more and more of my wine, the throb becomes more intense. Thought, which sometimes strikes you suddenly, is now impossible. I have this headache and a dull crampy feeling in my back, and under these circumstances wine becomes a cudgel, malleting my mind like a woman preparing veal cutlets. If it weren't for the strawberries and cream, I would leave.

"You know, Norma, you're very beautiful, in your own way. Especially now. At night. You should dwell in the night. It's your skin."

"I prefer natural light. I use it when I shoot."

"Do you like to make love in the daylight?"

I just look at him. I don't know what to do except pretend I'm deaf.

"Why do you evade me?" He says it as though we had been going on for weeks instead of hours. But my sense of time is protracted. My God, I'm tired. All the things that have happened today. All the walking and shopping and stuff. It seems that this day has been four. Maybe life for Corbett is like that too: quick meetings all over the city, talking to scores of people. God knows what he does for a living but it seems intense. Maybe time, for him, too, is a commodity without much meaning. "There must have been a reason for your coming to see me. You never told me. Is there something you need? Money? A place to stay? Maybe you're pregnant . . . ?"

"Um, Corbett, if there's one thing I'm *not* it's pregnant." I begin to wish against anything happening. *Please,* I pray, *don't let there be any stain on my new dress. You made me female, so don't embarrass me, O.K.?* It would happen tonight. To me. One of the few times I'm not wearing jeans, and I've got on a halfway decent dress, to blow my cool. The thought of my dress getting stained sort of *takes over,* and the only thing I want to do is to split for the john but then I need some Tampax which is up in my room which means that I've got to get to my room quickly and with the check and everything it's going to take forever and then Corbett would be there and then there's that bed and it'd be a big hassle.

My strawberries arrive. Corbett is having an apéritif instead.

"Would you like some, Corbett?" I ask, just being polite.

"No, thank you. Strawberries give me a rash in a rude place." He smiles smugly. "I would have said yes, if you offered me a cherry . . ."

Fortunately the bill arrives. Corbett is distracted. I split. Maybe you understand this. I don't. I can't exactly claim to be really thinking everything out. It's — well, you'd have to know Corbett, or someone like him. Or maybe you'd have to go through that thing with Joe, all that sticky possessiveness. And with Corbett, it's just that for once his eyes aren't hammering in on me and I just for once — maybe the only time in my life — want to cop out.

I think I am out the door before he is even out of his chair. I fly into the pension, snatch my key from its hook and run up the backstairs. My hand is shaking and I'm out of breath but I get the key in the lock and open the door and lock it behind me. I go over to the window and peek through the shutters. I start undressing. I can see Corbett down in the street, stand-ing outside the restaurant looking up the street and then down the other way. He gets into his car and drives off.

I push the little buzzer near my door. In a moment the owner's wife comes to the door. I wish I could tell someone about this. But I can't, my French isn't up to it. "Bain? S'il vous plaît . . . chaud . . ."

"Oui, Mademoiselle." She turns, then turns back. My face is flushed. "Ça va, Mademoiselle?"

I smile. "Oui . . . le vin . . ."

"Ahah . . ." She smiles approvingly and makes little circles with her upraised hand.

I get out my trench coat, which functions as a bath-robe, and my soap and the large bath towel she gave me this afternoon, a large fluffy one, bleached and puffed out. I glance at my small portable clock: 11:00. I get out my box of Tampax and a nightshirt and put everything else away.

If he figured it out, he'd be here by now, I say as I wander off to the tub.

FOURTEEN

I AM SOMEWHERE in yellow when I am awakened by a loud pounding far away. Then, when my eyes are opened and I find myself in the tub, dazed by the bare light bulb dangling overhead in the yellow enameled room, I hear a splintering crash. There is the rustle of nervous feet in the next room. Whispers of other guests behind their doors and the sounds of curious doors opening up an eyelash's breadth. I climb out of the tub and wrap myself in the towel. In goes the Tampax. Out goes the light and I open the door the same width as my neighbors'. The lights are on in my room. It is a dull light in a dull room. Forty-watt bulbs on twenty-watt green wallpaper. The owner's wife, in a bathrobe and slippers, her hair a bit scraggly, is shouting something at the man in my room. The light is so weak that it's only when he shouts back at her that I recognize Corbett's voice.

"Where is she?" He's pacing the room, opening up the wardrobe with such force that it must have snapped off its hinges. "Here's her dress. Her underwear is in the sink. She must have come in! Where are you hiding her? The little bitch! Where is she?"

"M'sieur. Je ne comprends pas. Qui . . ."

"Ma'mselle Cantalupo. Here are her cameras. Here are her clothes. This is her room. Où est-elle?" Then he says something in French which is harsh and authoritarian-sounding.

I am frightened for this lady who is doing all she can to stall. I'm not frightened for myself. Corbett doesn't seem to be in such a cool mood. I'm surprised he can get so angry. It seems out of character. Anyway, now that my head is clear and I've had my bath I may as well get it over with. I put on my nightshirt: an old white shirt of my father's from which I'd cut the collar and cuffs and tie dyed. And over that I put on my trench coat. I carry my towel, grip my door key, and stroll down the dark hall as if I'd heard nothing. Neither of them sees me until I'm in the room.

I place my hand on the lady's arm. "It's O.K. Merci. Ah . . . dix minutes, O.K.?"

"Bien. Monsieur. S'il vous plaît" — she raises her hand, one finger pointing upward — "*dix* minutes!"

Corbett nods. She leaves, closing the door behind her, though the lock is smashed.

Corbett turns on me. "Why did you run out on me like that? You don't have any idea . . ."

"Corbett — "

" — how I felt when you left — "

"Corbett — "

"I've been all over looking for you. I thought — I didn't know what to think — I — who do you think you are? I thought I could trust you — "

"Cor-bett!"

That stops him, at least.

"Sit down. I have something to tell you." Corbett sits on the bed, poaching his hurt. "I'm sorry. I didn't mean to upset you. I just didn't know what to do. I mean, nobody's ever told me the things you were telling me, and I'm not — I mean, I never thought of myself as being the, well, the seductive type. I'm sorry. I don't think — Look, let's put it this way, you're successful, well-off, divorced . . . I mean, I can't quite handle it. I'm just — " I stop. "Hey! How did you find me?"

"Easy. I have a friend who has a computer that knows where all American tourists sleep at night."

"O.K., you're political, too. I don't know anyone like you. You're scary. Don't you see? I mean, I'm just a kid from the Bronx. What do I know?"

He pulls me down next to him. "Who ever told you that?"

"What?"

"That stupid business about being just a kid from the Bronx."

"Well, nobody, but it's true."

"As we used to say, hogwash. You haven't seen much of the world, perhaps, but you will. You're not the type to wait for things to come to you. I've met only a few women like that, and most of them I don't think I liked very much because they kept trying to overreach their own limitations. But you've got something that goes beyond intelligence. It's a maternity of some kind. You'd make a good mother."

"Uh-oh. That sounds like Joe," I say.

"Joe?"

"A guy I dated for a long time. Until he started saying things like that."

Corbett takes out a cigarette. "You don't want to have children?"

I turn away to look at the door. "No. I don't want to get married, either."

"Well, that's fine. What's the fuss? But we could have beautiful children, you know. I'm not asking you to marry me. My psychiatrist won't let me, anyway."

"Let's look at it this way, Corbett. You've succeeded with your life. I haven't had a chance. If I go to bed with you or not isn't a big deal. But we're not equals. If I got involved with you — and I could — it wouldn't do me any good. It would be too much for me to handle. I think I'd much rather be alone. You can understand that, can't you . . ."

"Oh, yes. I certainly can. That's why I think you're wrong. I think I'm one of the very few men you could live with and still be free the way you want to be free. I wouldn't even mind other men."

"Then what's the point of being with you?"

"For my sake. I admit it. I'm a selfish man. I don't think anything could change you from what you are. Not money, not fame. There's a nice evenness about you. Perspective. You would help me a great deal. I want to retire and write books. You'd be a great asset. And I could help you get started."

"But I *am* started, Corbett. All on my own. Don't you see? I don't need your influence" — I pause to catch my breath — "or your money!"

"Oh. You don't?"

"No. And. And I have to go back home. I have people who care about me. Who I care about. Don't you think they're important to me?"

"Of course. Of course. But your ideals. Can you live up to them? Someone has to help you get going. Films cost money, no? Why is my money dirty? Money is money." He looks at my face for a moment. "We could have a lot of fun, you know, you and I. That's what being young is for." He says this softly.

We sit, saying nothing for a while. I sigh. "Can I think about all this? I mean, I'm not feeling well . . ."

"You're not?"

"No. Um, see those things in the sink? Well, during dinner I got my period all of a sudden. It was too complicated to explain and it would have taken so long. What I needed was to jump in the tub."

"I think it was more than that. I think it was what

I was saying. About coming to live with me. I think you're afraid of being a woman."

"That's not true." I begin to cry. "It can't be true." I start to laugh and cry. "I mean, I'm stuck, aren't I?"

He takes me in his arms and kisses my forehead and then my eyelids. "Listen, Norma. You're tired. Maybe you should think about this and I'll see you tomorrow and we can talk about it some more."

The proprietor's wife dutifully raps on the door. "Dix minutes, M'sieur."

"Oui." Corbett leans down and kisses my hands. "Bon soir," he says, leaving a little card on the night table next to the bed. "See you tomorrow."

Madame clears her throat.

FIFTEEN

I OVERSLEEP. I am awakened at around 10:30 by the roar of a metal screen — the kind that storekeepers shut over their shops at night. Through the cracks in the shutters of the window, the sun is sending yellow ribbons across my face.

I wash, dress, go to the john, and go downstairs to get some coffee into me. It is 11:00. Quel hangover. I study the card that Corbett gave me last night. For a little card it tells quite a story: "M. Paul C. Mason, Conseiller au Ministère des Affaires Economiques, République Française." There's a number engraved on it and an address. But there is also a penciled-in phone number with a circle around it which is, I gather, for me to use. I wonder how many others get to use the penciled number? I get my ally, Madame, the owner's wife, to dial the number for me. She is most sympathetic this morning. She first tells me that the secretary says that Monsieur Mason will return the call in a few minutes, and then Madame pours me a fresh pot of coffee and more newly warmed milk. She sits down with me at the small table.

I notice she has put all white daisies on the table. "Vous êtes triste?"

"Triste? Sad? Oui. Un peu."

"Monsieur . . . vous aimez?"

I can't figure out if she's saying, does he love me, or do I love him? And I'm not too sure if *aimer* means like or love or maybe to a Frenchman there's no difference but in this case it's sort of in between. "Oui," I say.

"Hier soir, quel accès de colère. Quel bouleversement! Je regrette . . ."

"Non. Mais non. Vous avez fait ce qu'il fallait." I'm not sure where I got that line. Maybe an old French movie line: *You have done what must be done.* Early Michele Morgan, maybe.

The phone rings. Madame answers. "Pour vous . . ."

"Merci," I say, smiling. I go over to the phone. But the voice isn't Corbett's and my smile cools.

"A-loo. M'sieur Mason ask me to call you to tell you zat 'e is sorry but 'e haz flight to Londres. 'E vould like you to call 'imm tonight at seven-teen hours. Comprenez-vous? Seven-teen hours. Do you have 'ees phone num-bear?"

"At the Ritz Hotel?"

"Non. Ici. 'Ere."

"Yes, I do."

"All right. Seven-teen hours. Good-bye."

"Au revoir."

I don't know what to do. I go up to my room, fill my purse with Tampax, and head out for American Express.

SIXTEEN

NORM CANTALUPO PAR

MEET ME MILAN AIRPORT   ALITALIA

#431 1:35 PM JULY 2   URGENT

ANDREA

Peculiar. Very. Only five days. I don't have much choice. I pick up my $100 N.A.S.A. check and change it into traveler's checks. I won't need it for a long time, fortunately. I can't leave Andrea stranded in Milan. I can't stay here, either. I need time to think about Corbett. He certainly can live without me. Flying to London, eh? Just slipped his mind. Well, as Washington once said, "Avoid entangling foreign alliances."

I go to wire Andrea a reply.

SEVENTEEN

I GUESS it's the jeans. I mean, if I thought that there would be all these other slobs here maybe I wouldn't have come. But here I am at Versailles because it's my last day. It was a choice between Versailles and Chartres. I wish I had gone to Chartres. There are a lot of people here. All slobs, like me. The mirrors reflect us. Hordes of slobs. Except for a few well-dressed people who clump together as if they were afraid the barbarians might turn on them.

All this gilt and marble and the paintings and the draperies. It all sort of turns me off. The world remembers Marie Antoinette for one thing: for being a foolish woman. A loser. If she had died naturally — in childbirth even, she had kids — but she didn't. She lived to be toppled off her pedestal. And now that she's long dead, the same kind of people who delighted in her ignominious end, the descendants of Madame DeFarge you might say, are gumshoeing it around her palace. All accidents of birth, these women we remember. Queens, courtesans, and saints. And this stuff about motherhood Corbett was giving me last night. Bullshit. History never remembered a woman simply because she was a good mother.

I go out into the garden. All that gold leaf was making me dizzy. The gardens are vast and dull green in color and relaxing. There are pebble paths. I sit down to watch some tiny brown birds play in a small puddle of rainwater.

I wonder if the insurance will cover it. My mother's operation, that is. Was it really only three weeks ago when we had that fight?

"Joe called," she said as soon as I walked into the kitchen.

"Yeah?" I said, putting the kettle on to boil. "Want some tea?"

"Thanks. You're not going to call him back?"

"Why should I?" I got some cups out.

"But it's the fourth time he's called."

"Yeah." I got the teapot out and dropped in two teaspoons of Lipton's.

"Aren't you and he . . . ?"

"No."

"But why not? Joe's a nice boy. He'll be a good husband. I can tell."

"How can you tell?" The kettle whistled.

"Believe me. I've seen them all. There were five of us girls at home. We all had boy friends. I had some boy friends too, you know. But I could tell the good ones from the bad ones. I knew your Aunt Paula would regret marrying Tom. I knew that your father was right for me, though." She looked up at me. "Don't let it steep too long, Norma."

"Yes, Mother." I sat down opposite her.

"You'll be out of school soon. Joe's finishing up his night-school classes. He's got a job already. Ambitious. Tells your father he wants to get his engineering degree next."

"You wanta get rid of me, Ma?"

"No, baby. It's just that . . . I like Joe. He's what your father would have been if it weren't for the war. He should have gone to school when he got out. But things were different then. Life got postponed for so long that school just wasn't for him. But Joe . . . He's so nice."

"Right, Ma. He's nice. *Nice*. You know what nice is? It's a word you use to describe someone who has nothing going for him. If you fix somebody up with a blind date, you say, 'He's nice,' which means, 'He's a little shorter than you are, but you should be glad you've got a date Saturday.'"

"Norma . . . He's got some good qualities. He's kind. He doesn't have a temper, does he? Does he sneak around with other girls behind your back? Doesn't he bring you presents?"

"Yeah, he brings me presents, all right. And you flowers, and Richie records, and Dad some bootleg Havanas every once in a while. He's buying me. What's your price? Thirty shekels?"

"Norma! I bet you never think of the future. Don't you think that in-laws make a difference? Joe's parents are our friends. We get along. They think of you as a daughter. It's important to have good feelings on both sides."

"All right, Mama. Why don't you and Dad and the Ragusas hire a lawyer and draw up a marriage contract. It'll make everyone happy except me!" I was crying.

"Oh, baby, don't. I don't understand. I mean, when you get to be my age you realize . . ."

"Mama. I'm not your age, thank God. And my horizon is a lot wider than Fordham Road and Jerome Avenue! And I don't want to spend the rest of my life making spaghetti and picking up socks and washing diapers and drinking coffee all morning with my friends . . ."

"Norma! Norma Maria! Now you listen to me! When and if you get to be my age, you will be on your knees every night thanking God that He gave you a faithful husband and decent children and any friends at all to share your joys and sorrows. There are worse things in life than being Joe Ragusa's wife! You go to Europe. Do what you have to do. Get this — this romantic stuff — out of your system. But when you come back you'd better decide. You can't step on the people who love you. Don't think I'll let you do that to me. I have nothing to gain by what you decide to do with your life except knowing that you're happy. No one's forcing you to marry Joe. But I challenge you to find someone better!"

Then we could hear Papa and Richie coming up the stairs, Richie bouncing his basketball the way that Old Man Giardina downstairs finds so endearing and Papa whistling "Volare."

"Go wash your face, Norma," Mama said, blowing her nose into her handkerchief and turning on the gas jet under the big pot filled with water.

EIGHTEEN

IT IS getting dark when I arrive at my pension. I'm tired and gritty. At least I've come to some kind of a compromise. Versailles teaches you that.

I'm right. That's number one. Marrying Joe isn't it. My mother is right. That's number two. I won't find anyone better than Joe. And Corbett is right. Life is to be lived. That's number three. But as to fitting them all together into a path of action, I can't.

I mean, maybe all those years in parochial school were a big waste. 'Cause like I think I'm a Lutheran at heart. Predestination. It never occurred to me that I might have some control over my life. That right now I could decide to live with Corbett. Or I could decide to go back home. I mean, I don't think I'm capable of living with Corbett, of hurting my parents. But I don't think I'm capable of shutting myself off by marrying Joe. Or anyone, for that matter. Or maybe Corbett is right. Maybe what I want is to marry Joe and to have lots of kids but I'm afraid I'll fail at that. And then where will I be? Why can't someone decide for me?

It's seven o'clock. Since I said I would call him, I'd better call. I dial his office number. It rings over and over and over. There's no answer. Then I dial the hotel. I push button A, the desk clerk, Mister Mouse, answers. I push button B.

"Monsieur Mason? Paul Mason?"

"I am sorry. M'sieur Mason has left word that he will be gone for two days. If it is urgent he said he can be reached at the French Embassy in London. Is there a message?"

"No," I say, hanging up. Damn, damn, damn.

NINETEEN

I AM TOO ANGRY TO CRY. I start packing instead.
There's not much. A few sweaters, a couple of knitted
shirts, shoes. What's left — comb and brush and de-
odorant — I can stuff into some corner tomorrow morning.

Though I'm not hungry, I decide to go for a walk
and then work up an appetite and have a farewell
platter of coquilles, even though the thought of it almost makes me ill.

If I were a man and he were a woman, what would
I do? Probably I wouldn't care. Or I would care but
I wouldn't say anything. I'd just go away. Or I'd go
and find him. But I can't do that. I'm stuck. Again.
Or maybe even a guy couldn't eat this kind of shit.

I go down the street, down the block, around the

bend. I stop in a small square and there are some people singing and some people sitting in the café. I stand there for a while and then go back to my little restaurant.

There's almost no one there. As soon as I come in the doorway, the waiter comes over and says something about "votre ami," but I am so distracted that I think he's just saying something about last night or where is my friend tonight or something like that. Or maybe he's saying *he* is my friend.

"Coquilles?" I say.

"Rien, Mademoiselle. Je le regrette." But he leads me to a table and sits me down and in a few seconds is back with a platter of a mixture of things: snails, tomatoes, eggs, olives. And he brings a bowl of soup next. And a little later he brings strawberries. I notice that the bill is quite low tonight. Maybe the cook went home. It's awfully late. So I leave a very large tip and shake hands with everyone and tell them I'm leaving Paris but that I'll see them again someday. You may not believe me, but it really was quite touching.

When I reach for my key, the proprietor of my pension eyes me suspiciously. "Bon soir," I say.

"Bon soir," he replies.

I can't think of the right words. "De bonne heure, demain. Je partirai Paris. Au Marseille. Faites-vous le compte?" I get something across, that is certain. But rather than reply he hands me an envelope. At first I think it's the bill. Then I see it's not. It's a letter. It could only be from one person.

I run up the dark stairway. The envelope in my hand, being of a textured paper, speaks of taste and experience and integrity.

In my room, I open up the letter. The clock has stopped at 9:30.

My dearest Norma,

You can't imagine what a terrible day this has been. I was called away to London early this morning on urgent business. I hadn't time to talk to you, and I'm sorry that I couldn't call you right back, but there were last-minute briefings I had to attend. But I knew that there was a flight I could get on tonight and so I had my secretary tell you to call back at 5. Perhaps you misunderstood. Anyway, I was back at 4:30, I called you, waited for you to call, drove up to your little hotel, waited an hour for you and finally I had to leave because there were more meetings in London late tonight. (Do you realize that I kept all these important people waiting just for you!)

Where did you go? Why didn't you come back? Your concierge there thinks she's doing you a favor by not telling me anything. She told me she thinks I'm a nuisance. Why didn't you call me?

Who were you out with? That French fellow? I even went to the restaurant next door.

Perhaps I used the wrong approach. Have you had enough time to think? Was that what you were doing all day? Is your disappearance your reply?

I have only enough time to make my flight to London. You see, I'm not capable of having confining relationships, either. My job is too exhausting. There's no question of your freedom.

Please don't run away from me again.

Love, Corbett

Andrea expects me in Milan and Corbett expects me to stay here. Well, Corbett can manage to find me or I him, but Andrea isn't quite as capable and she probably needs me to get her around. And *she* said urgent.

Dear Corbett,

I'm terribly sorry about today. I guess I'm still confused about European time. Your secretary said 17 hours and I thought that meant 7 o'clock, so I went out to Versailles and I didn't come back until around 6:30. I'm very sorry that I didn't see you because I have been thinking about last night and about a lot of other things. To be honest, I'm more confused than ever. I won't be here when you get back but it's just because I have to go first to Marseille and then to Milan. I still have to do several interviews and I got a telegram from someone asking me to meet her at Milan on the 2nd. You can write to me in care of American Express there. And I should be back here in a few weeks before going to Amsterdam for the flight back. I do think that whatever I do with my life I should finish school first. Don't you agree? And my mother isn't well and I may have to run the house for a while. But I do want to see you again. You'll be in New York won't you? My phone number there is: 443-5596. I'm not running away from you — just doing more thinking.

Love, Norma

TWENTY

MARSEILLE. The station is large and squared off. Square marble pillars. Square slabs on the floor. Modern, that is to say in a twenties way. The color of the interior, which is a beige-rust, does not quite prepare me for the sharp snap of sunlight outside. I cross a parking lot or taxi stand and find I am up on a terraced hill. The city is there at my feet. It's incredible. I imagine I can see the port, though it's a fuzzy mirage, I think. There are stairs, à la *Potemkin*, down to the street.

It's a long way down. On the right, on one of the landings, is a small café. I walk down, gear and all. These two guys in short-sleeved white shirts and baggy pants and saddle shoes and sunglasses have Polaroids

hung around their necks. They are debating something. I take a few more steps down and the taller and
thinner one runs up to me, takes my picture, and then
smiles. He waits for me to come closer. He says something about twenty francs. I shake my head and keep
walking. Fifteen francs, he says. I decide to keep going
and not to look. Ten Francs he shouts. When I'm at
about the bottom he gives up and goes back to the shorter
and fatter one to bitch about me.

Directly ahead of me is a broad street. The side-
walks are shaded by trees and awnings. Still, it is
warm. And the people look different. Paris was cool
and still. Here it is really summer. And it gives me the
feeling that it must always be warm here, that the sun
must be always bright and that it couldn't rain or be
gray.

I am accustomed now to finding the American Express office in the most logical places. In Marseille it
is the same. I almost pass it without noticing, but then
the logicality of its location strikes me and, rather than
see it, I know it should be where it is. Inside it is as
absurdly cold as an American movie theater in summer.
I lower my equipment gently to the floor and in my
knapsack I find my passport. I wait on a short line
and soon my hand is warmed by two envelopes. One
is my check from N.A.S.A. plus a memo to call Marco
at 34–755. I'm beginning to wonder if any of my
contacts have last names.

The other bears my own address on the back flap.
I barely recognize my father's handwriting. I sit down

on a little bench to read it, my gear scattered on the floor around my feet like nursery-school children. I finger the envelope and speculate that it says to come home on the next plane because Mama is blind and she needs me. This is what I have been thinking about for the past seven hours when I was on the train, and what has been in my dreams these past nights. I've been thinking how meaningless this trip is in relation to Mama's blindness. How selfish I am. It's been a bad seven hours. And now the letter.

Dear Norma,

Hope you are having a good time and that your film is coming along well. Here is $50 (I bet on a winner this time) for you to buy your mother something pretty. Maybe a purse or a dress or something. You know what she would like better than me. Got your postcards. Send more. And don't forget to look up those people I told you about in Palermo. Nothing's new here. It's hot. When you come back maybe we'll go up to the mountains. Have fun.

Love, Dad

Well. It's not what I'd expected. Not really. But he should have known that I'd see through it. I mean, since when does he write letters to me? It's always Mom. Like those three summers when Richie and I stayed with Uncle Mike and Aunt Lucy up in Putnam County. And the time Mom and Dad went on an anniversary trip for two weeks to Florida. And who does he think he's fooling? Nothing's new except the weather is hot! My ass. Somewhere along the line somebody had a baby and somebody got sick and went to the hospital and somebody just got out of the army. I mean, with all our cousins and neighbors and friends from school, there's an awful lot of somebodies. And somebody's always having something happen to them, or to their friends or to their parents or to their children. I mean, when nothing's new, it's a lie.

Something's wrong. Of course, he doesn't know that Richie wrote me. But still. He could have said she had an operation and that everything is fine. He could have said: *And Mom sends her love, too,* which Mom always said Dad sent us at the end of her letters. I mean, I'm sure something's terribly wrong. I'll be seeing Andrea; maybe that'll help clear things up.

TWENTY-ONE

THE HOTEL ROOM is clean and modern and entirely too expensive and extremely small. But it does have one advantage. It's so small that when Marco and his two friends get here, there's no room to move around.

"Marco? I'm afraid there's not enough room. Can't we go someplace else?" I ask, anxious to get the three of them out of here.

"Oh, oui. Of course. Louis?"

"That's all right."

"Paul?"

"Fine."

"Where can we go, Marco?"

"To my villa. It's not far."

Shooting at night presents some problems, but I do

have some special slow-speed film which may help the lighting situation. We pack ourselves into a small dark car. It reminds me of Michele's car. In fact there's that old problem again of fitting my gear into the trunk. Well, it's these cars.

I'm not sure that this going out to the villa is any better than staying in my room, but, first, it would have been technically impossible to shoot three people in such a small space and, second, Paul (or was it Louis?) was reading this really gross magazine and he has that kind of stupid face that parents frighten children into thinking they'll get if they continue masturbating.

We drive along one street, a narrow one which is filled with people — mostly an assortment of tough prostitutes à la *Playboy* cartoons. Then, suddenly, out out of the bazaar — human and trinket type — we come to the port. Marco wants me to see it. More people. More Arabs and prostitutes and sailors. And tourists thinking how exotic it all is. Then we follow a road which runs along the shore. We go about three miles then take another road, straight up the hill and then along another tiny lane until we come to the villa. It is surrounded by a wall and in the corner, next to the gate, is a small tower. When I first see it I think it is a flag post that's jutting out of the window. Then over it I see a face silhouetted in the evening light. And when I think about it for a moment, I decide the flag post is a rifle.

Marco is leading me around the garden to a back door. There seem to be a lot of trees. Marco tells me they're apricots. "It's a shame you couldn't come during the day. The view from up here is superb. You can see the entire city and a little bit of the sea. You can see the Château d'If and, on a clear day, the Basilica of Notre Dame de la Garde."

Inside the house were marble and polished-wood floors which weren't so polished and glass chandeliers covered with spiderwebs and dust. The furniture was all wrong for the place and the light was dim. It was spooky. I don't want to bore you with details. Suffice it to say it was creepy and that after setting up my sound equipment for me Paul (or was it Louis?) disappeared, which left Marco, who was really my contact and not the subject I needed for the documentary. Then Louis (or was it Paul?) decided to keep on reading his book and masturbating, so I couldn't exactly film him and after a few shots I put everything away. There wasn't much on the film except profiles and the book jacket.

Marco drives me back, apologizing all the way.

I don't even get undressed when I get back to my room. I just sack out. In the morning I look like an old potato that's been in the back of the drawer for four months.

TWENTY-TWO

On THE TRAIN I am reading a book. Something that Marco gave me last night. There was a stack of them in the corner of one of the rooms. Marco found me an English translation. It's entitled *The Call to Revolution* by the People's Writing Committee. It's a collective effort, obviously. The cover is red, obviously. It makes no sense, obviously. Take this chapter on art and society. Now, I'm not sure that what I'm doing, this making films, is art. I mean, I'm not calling myself an artist, but my film won that prize over a lot of artsy-craftsy types so I guess that my sense of reality is an artistic one. So what this committee wants to say is that art has no function in a revolutionary society because art is always elitist, meaning that whatever artists do they want recognition. I'll drink to that. Generally you die, you know, and, after a few years, the only people around to remember you are your children if you have any or your friends and then they die and so no one remembers you at all. I think I'd like some recognition, thank you.

I put down this book to gaze out the window at the long long sea. I'd been half expecting it to disappear. I don't know why. But I kind of thought it would. We go through Monaco, a strippy kind of city; I wish I could lean out and grab some of it.

The water continues. The whole railway line seems to be a beach with towns plunked down and now there's a tunnel. When we get out of the tunnel we stop. Out of nowhere come these customs officials. First French, then Italian. There *is* a difference. The Italians are smiling in a perfunctory way, perhaps, but they are smiling, as if, maybe fifteen years ago when they first started their jobs on the trains, they might have said "Welcome to Italy," but that they've said it so many times, the only thing that's left is the pale shadow of a welcome. Also, they tip their caps to me. This is a country where being the object of male chauvinism has its own rewards. "Signorina, grazie," they say as they hand me back my passport.

As the train pulls forward, my blood starts to perk. *Italy*, something is whispering inside. *Italy*. I can remember Nonna, her sturdy black shoes tightly laced and planted on the tile floor, the rest of her towering over me like a large gingham hill, her head bent over the sink and I can hear the melody and some of the words were "Italia, la bella . . ." Maybe even she had forgotten the words after so many years in the Bronx.

And then there was Nonno, a large brown cigar always, his leathery hand, a tailor's hand, on my cheek, the way his round head with its thick fringe of white hair would shine under the bright chandelier over the heavy oak table where we would eat dinner on Sundays in their apartment. How his white mustache would move when he spoke English, slowly like a child, and how rapidly it would go when he spoke Italian and how his hands would dance then. And how he drew on his cigar. And how he smelled: a blend of soap and Havana tobacco. The stories he used to tell me of the day my father was born. The celebrations they had. The dancing. Their friends. And I remember his summer garden in the lot in the Bronx where there are now two two-family brick houses. But in summer we would go there and its color was green. Pure green. And the earth was moist all the time from Nonno's watering can. And I can see cousin Elizabeth and me taking baths and running in our underpants through the trees. It's all so long ago. I seem to remember a dog, too, but I'm not sure of that.

But out the window. It's here. I can see it. I can see it.

TWENTY-THREE

I HAVE only two hours in Turin. Two hours. It is almost dusk. When I get out of the station I realize that the station itself is an introduction to the city. The arches begin inside. Having checked my baggage, I guess I can manage to put it back on board myself without much fuss. I walk outside and from behind the pillars I sense that the arches have leapfrogged across the street and that they are running around Turin. So I chase them.

Not only is the city like a big arcaded shopping center, but just as I start crossing the street to see some of the shops along the way, the lights go on. It's very distracting, you know. I mean, I always take it personally no matter where I am when it happens. So along with the old-fashioned streetlamps, on go the neon signs.

I notice that I must be walking the wrong way because all of the signs face the wrong way. It's hard to describe, but like at home neon signs go flat against the wall, right? In Italy they're made funny. They stick out. I mean like perpendicularly. So every one of them faces away from me and I can't read a letter. It's like looking at Times Square done up in Hebrew. But I look over my shoulder and behind me everything's O.K. So what the signs are really saying is "Ciao," I guess. For when you're leaving.

There are lots of people sitting in the cafés. Businesses are probably closed by now, though the shops are open. I pass shoe stores and men's clothing stores and jewelry stores and fabric stores. One restaurant is like a 1890s gem. Its doors are opened and you can see the wallpaper of watery ladies done up in pearly sea gowns. I myself am out of place in my jeans and knitted shirt. I might as well have on a set of Mickey Mouse ears. I turn a corner and go down a rounded area. There's a newsstand and nearby there's a young boy selling lottery tickets. I can tell because lottery tickets and lottery ticket buyers are all the same. They always have that pained look on their faces of people who have lost and always will lose but who are cynical enough to keep trying. The piazza is broad and the streets come together in a lazy way.

Everyone is talking. But they all look as if they are really talking about something *important*. Not just about the football game or about the new car they're about to buy. They are talking about what really bothers them. Politics, maybe. The economy. I walk behind two middle-aged men. They are both stout like old trees. Despite the iridescent glare of the lights and the neon signs, the men look tan and in pretty good health, though the one on the left walks with a slight limp. The one on the right holds his friend's arm while he's talking. The one on the left is walking with his hands clasped behind him. While the other talks, making small pirouettes with his hands, the one on the left suddenly lifts his right arm and places it on his friend's shoulder and begins to talk with great feeling in his voice. They're not making those dumb TV-comedian kind of gestures but exquisite punctuations. Like a Hawaiian hula, really, saying: *But, my friend, you know how these things are, how it's always men like you and me who suffer.* The one on the right puts his arm on his friend's back. Abruptly they stop and face each other, talking. I have to stop too and I try to go around them. But the stop, like the gestures, is merely a punctuation mark: an emphatic one, however. They walk on quickly and I stop in a Motta café to see what is inside.

It's unique, I'll grant you that. Kind of like a cross between the old Schrafft's and a cafeteria. There are tables inside and outside and then places to stand and eat. I get some food by pointing. My favorite method. And after I pay for it some guy by the door points me back to the counter. "Signorina . . . consumi dentro per piacere . . ."

"Huh?" I reply.

"Dentro."

So I end up sipping my espresso and eating an emaciated ham sandwich standing at the counter. I plan to have dinner in Milan, anyway, I tell myself.

When I finish, it is dark and most of the people are gone from the streets. Just as I'm about to go, a very timid lady with a charming face stops me.

"Excuse me, but can you help me?" She is quite frail-looking. Her British accent, though, is strong.

"Sure. What can I do?"

"Well, I suspected that you spoke English and I do need to find the, ah, powder room. Do you happen to know where I could find it?"

"I have found," I said, taking her elbow, "that ladies' rooms are usually next to the men's rooms and that would be upstairs, I think. I've seen several guys — er — gentlemen going up and coming down over there. Shall we go?"

"Oh, if it's not too much trouble for you. You see, sometimes I have trouble getting up stairs."

And after all that was taken care of, this little lady and I had some tea and we talked about Italy and her musical training as a young girl and her admiration for the spirit of Italian musicianship and about her fiancé who was killed in World War I and the way he used to play his violin for her while she played the piano and a third friend sang.

It was a lovely conversation and I hated to go, but I didn't want to miss the train. I hope she finds her way to wherever she's going next.

TWENTY-FOUR

So far, my train rides have been mostly a chance to read or to make notes on my interviews or to make drawings of stuff I want to remember. But it's hard to do much of anything when so much is going on. I mean, not a lot of entertaining stuff, but people stuff.

There is a woman sitting by the window in the seat diagonally opposite me. Her eyes are open but I think she's asleep because there's nothing to see except a black landscape with maybe a few lights every time we speed through a town. Or maybe she's thinking about something. Her eyes hardly blink. Next to me, opposite her, is her eight-year-old daughter, definitely asleep, curled over a little like a small cat.

We are only a few miles out of Turin, the train

lurching around towns and under hills and stuff, and it's not possible to write, actually. I'm more or less relieved when a young man, about twenty-five years old, stops by me in the aisle, his ticket in hand.

He looks at me. I look at him.

"Signorina . . ." and then he says something which I can't quite understand.

"Je ne comprends pas," I say like a jerk in French. "Parlez-vous anglais?"

"An-glis? Si. Un poco. That chair . . . she is mine."

"Impossible," I say, shaking my head.

"Signorina . . ." He's obviously an impatient man who is restraining himself. He smiles. "Is riservato . . . (*Tte.*) Come si dice? (*Tte.*) Reserved? Per me. (*Tte.*) Vede?"

I look at his ticket. Then he looks at my ticket.

"See?"

"Si-si. (*Tte.*)"

The conductor arrives. In rapid Italian the situation is discussed. Much nodding and *Tte*ing and *Prego*ing is all I can catch. It's a little like taxation without representation.

"You see," the conductor says, bending over as if in a protracted bow, "the computer made a mistake. Your ticket is from Torino, no? This gentleman's ticket was obtained in Savona. It's a very small mistake. You made your reservations at the same time. But these things are the problems of our modern age. It's not so important where you sit. The other seat is not taken and this is diretto to Milano, so there should be no problem. My apologies, Signorina, for the inconvenience." He rises and tells the young man to sit across from me. He accompanies his directive with an exasperated look, as if to suggest that this guy was upsetting his liver and that anyone with initiative would not have made so much fuss.

The young man sits down. Sitting right in front of me, staring, his fine cheekbones standing out, his nose flared in annoyance. I turn to the darkened window and watch him study me. The straight nose reflects the straight zigzag edges of his white shirt, collar spread at the neck and the sandy silk-tweed jacket collar. I notice that his eyes are greenish blue to match the silk handkerchief in his pocket and that his trousers are the exact color of his well-cut hair. He's staring at me. First at my face and hair, then at my jeans then back at my face then back at my jeans.

A girl about my age gets up in the other end of the car. I watch her as she comes down the aisle toward me. As she passes I watch his reaction. He turns slightly and without a blink stares after her. Her walk is interesting. A nice combination of Dominique Sanda and Garbo. Her dress is knitted with a kinky butterfly design front-and-center on the top and on the side of the skirt. She sports a nice suede purse the exact color of the butterfly and shoes to match, and around her throat she's got a choker with a small red butterfly which could have been painted with the same nail polish on her finger tips and toes and her eye shadow is violet, mauve, and purple to go with the rest of her. After an appropriate interim, she saunters back down the aisle with a glass of something in her hand. He watches her intently, so intently you would think she'd trip, and she passes and he turns to see where she sits down and I expect *something* to happen, but it doesn't. And we continue, this guy staring at my jeans and I at the window for another hour or so until we reach Milan.

As the train slows down and comes to a halt, the sleeping mother and child awaken. I am already on my feet, collecting my knapsack and baggage receipts. The woman awakens, nods her dark head at me, offers her hand to shake, which I take, prods her daughter who shakes my hand too, we say "Ciao," we nod, and when I turn around to nod again they've both gone back to sleep and I lump and bump my way down the aisle and down onto the platform.

If Turin had arches beginning in the train station and running through the city, Milan has hugeness. The ceiling, if that's what you can call it, is up in heaven someplace. People are on the platform caressing each other, leaping into each other's arms, singing. There are lots and lots of children and babies, but they always turn up at airports even at home so it's not a surprise. What's surprising is that they're all in relatively good moods, at this hour of the night. One little child, barely able to stand, much less walk, toddles in front of me before I see her. She falls over, her little skirt up, her hands out in front of her round little head.

I stop to see if I can help her up but she's up in a second. I look up at the mother who is laughing. She picks up the child. "I'm sorry," I say. She smiles and nods as if to say, *It's not the first time and certainly not the last.* I hesitate, wanting to ask her something. I don't know why. Something about Dr. Spock. About breast-feeding, about toilet-training. Things I know nothing about. In her laugh I can hear that she knows everything I need to know. "I'm sorry," I say walking away.

Just ahead of me the chick on the train with the butterflies is walking arm in arm with an older woman also nicely knitted together. They are both tan and are carrying straw bags stuffed with clothes and towels. Ahead of them and to one side, about ten yards away, is the Young Man I was telling you about before. Butterfly nudges Mama, who turns to look at Y.M., who slows his pace somewhat coincidentally, and the two ladies speed it up a bit and, what do you know! Before long they are slightly ahead of Y.M., who pauses and nods, and they stop and, whammo, he's carrying two straw bags and chatting and the ladies are giggling and I lose them when I stop to collect the rest of my gear from the baggage car.

TWENTY-FIVE

You've got to hand it to him, that Arthur Frommer.
I mean, he can get you out of a train in the middle of
a strange city in the middle of the night and give you
the insane idea that it's a snap to get a hotel room or
find a restaurant. I mean, me and every other American who got off that train is a *Five Dollars a Day*
thumper. My cabbie is driving me through beautiful
downtown Milan, which is a funny expression but
Milan may be the only city I've been to where that
applies. I mean, even at night Milan has a downtown
and it looks great. Big broad streets, trees silhouetted,
tall buildings, trolleys, buses, traffic, ancient structures
thrown in every once in a while.

After about ten minutes we come to a pointy hulk

lit up. I roll down the window and lean out to take a better look.

"The Duomo?" I ask the cab driver.

"Si. Hey. You American?" He asks in basic Brooklynese. "You gotta see dat church, girl. It's terrif'. Beeeu-ti-ful."

"You from America?" I ask.

"Me? Naw. I was born here. Got to the US courtesy of a POW boat. But I had some relatives and somebody put a fix on some papers for me and I stayed, married an American girl. Those are my kids up there." He switches on the light momentarily and I catch a glimpse of a photo of four toothy kids paperclipped to his sun shield. "You from New York?"

"Yes."

"Where?"

"The Bronx."

"Bronx! Hey. Terrif'." He stops for a light. "Listen, why you goin' to Il Parigi?"

"Because I heard it was a good hotel." I hold up *Five Dollars a Day*.

"Ah. Dat book! Look. I'll take you to a place beddah dan dat and cheapeh." The light changes. "Look, I use to live in da Bronx."

"How come you decided to come back?"

"Well, t'ings dinnt work out. For a time I was workin' out in Brooklyn at da Navy Yard, den dat close, den somebody give me a job in da Bronx in construction. But den 'bout eight years ago my papa died, see, and lef' me a nice house here. Ya know, if I hadn't been in da army and been a prisoner I would of gone to da university here like my brother. Lodda good it did him when he got shot. One t'ing 'bout Americans. Don't know nottin' 'bout war. Don't know how it destroys people. When we lef' it was Vietnam. I says to my wife at leas' in Italy we don't have no rent to pay, no insurance premiums like dat damn Blue Cross."

"How's life for you here?"

"I drive a cab, miss, but you know what I'm doin'? I'm writin' a book."

"Very good!"

"Hey, you know, I didn't pick you for American. Thought you were British. Maybe . . . German? Take da average Italian girl, you know she'd never wear jeans. Not ever. Unless she's really rich. Don't get too many from da Bronx. Mostly from Lon-Giland. Got relatives here?"

"No. Not here. In Palermo, some."

"Palermo? Ah. Siciliana! You gonna go visit? You should, you know. There's no place on earth so beeu-ti-ful as Sicily!"

"Where are you taking me?"

"To dis place my friend runs. He'll give you a break 'cause he's my friend."

"Does he serve breakfast?"

"Breakfast? Listen, miss, Italians don't really know about breakfasts. Dey t'ink if you eat an egg in da morn-ing you'll explode. If you want a good breakfast go to a restaurant. Here we are." He stops and then helps me out of the cab. The street is narrow and dim and a little creepy, but the lobby of the hotel is bright and clean and the ceilings have old paintings on them. The cab driver yells out, "Franco! Fran-co," as we walk through the door and proceeds to translate my needs to his friend, tells me the price, helps me with the baggage, and tells me what I owe him. His fee comes to 2000 lire, which I figure is too much, but he was worth it and the hotel is certainly something dear Arthur would never share with the world if he ever knew about it.

TWENTY-SIX

Hot town,
summer in the city,
Back o' my neck
gettin' dirt and gritty.
Been down,
isn't it a pity;
Doesn't seem to be a shadow in the city.
All around people lookin' half dead,
Walkin' on the sidewalk
hotter than a matchhead.

Cappuccino, croissants, a glass of freshly squeezed orange juice, plastic ribbons in the door, five tables, people stopping by for a quick cup of espresso, John Sebastian crooning lovingly out of the jukebox. I have four more hours to kill. I have to go to meet Andrea at the airport. Milan. Man, New York filled with Italians. The Italian version of the Work Ethic.

Having paid the lady for my coffee, I walk over to the Duomo. The pensione owner penciled in the streets I should take to get there. It's not far and I manage to find it after a few blocks. It's the Milanese Arc de Triomphe. I mean, to get to it you have to go down these stairs and under the piazza or you could take your chances and cross the streets. I don't know what to do, but I see a gaggle of German tourists ahead of me, so I decide to follow them. The tunnel is a surprise. No rude graffiti or peeling ads. There are display cases and a subterranean entrance to a department store like the one at the 59th Street IRT stop into Bloomingdale's.

The cathedral looks kind of like a cave of huge stalagmites like Ausable Chasm, or wherever it was that we went when I was ten years old. In front of the church is a big square which is mostly filled with pigeons being fed through the courtesy and profit of some lady in a cotton dress and a straw hat with an umbrella stand on wheels which bears a sign which I can't read but she's selling the seeds to the tune of fifty lire per bag.

I discover that my vibrations are in order this morning. To impress Andrea I put on my new gray dress, even though I'm sweltering. So when I go into the cathedral through the huge doors, I see this little man giving some American chicks in hot pants a hard time.

About all he can do is point indignantly at their bare thighs. They don't understand him, that he's trying to prevent them from going inside because they're indecent.

"But you don't under*stand*," the skinnier girl is saying. "All my luggage is in the ho*tel*, and the tour is going to leave in an *hour* for Rome and we can't go back and *change*. I mean the only thing we came to see in Milan is this church and I'm not going to leave without *see*ing it. You can't *do* this. I mean we're A*mer*ican *cit*izens! Look, we paid all this *mon*ey to see Italy and now you won't let us go in*side*. I mean I don't under*stand*."

"Signorina, I am very sorry. You cannot go inside . . ."

"What's he saying, Louise?"

"I don't know. I think he's speaking I*tal*ian."

". . . with short pants. Mi dispiace. It is proibito. Prohibited."

"I *think* he's saying we can't go inside because we have *shorts* on. He says it's pro*hib*ited."

"Oh. I didn't understand him at all. Ask him what about those guys over there. I mean if they can go in, why can't we?"

"Listen, mister. Those boys over *there*" — Louise points — "they have shorts on. Why can they go in and not us? Don't you *want* Americans in your church?"

"Come on, Louise . . ."

"No, Margo! I want to see this church. We *paid*

for the tour and I want to *see* it. We're not leaving until we do!" She points again at what looks to me like a Boy Scout troop. "Why can *they* go in and not us?"

"Signorina" — he spreads his hands, palms up, thumbs traveling east and west — "they are boys. You are girls. Women are not permitted to display their — ah — limbs. Shoulders, legs. *Tte.*" He shakes his head. (I've figured out by now that this *Tte* is a sound meaning something quite negative.) For a little man paid to watch hemlines and bare shoulders all day, he is incredibly cool to watch.

"Well!" Louise exclaims. "I've never *heard* of anything so stupid!"

"What did he say, Louise?"

"He said that it's O.K. for them because they're boys. Come on, Margo, let's go!" Louise spins around and brushes past me. She turns as she walks and yells, "Male chauvinist pig!"

I regain my balance (Louise brushes hard) and turn to the little man, who is gazing discreetly at the backs of their legs. He turns to me and shrugs. He's obviously not angry. There's no trace of a smile. If he were a sophisticated man he might even be amused. But that seems out of character. He's just doing his job.

TWENTY-SEVEN

THAT WAS the most awful experience I ever had. Norm, don't you agree? Isn't flying just awful? I have this terrible migraine and my legs are hurting. I had a headache for six hours! And that baby! If only that baby weren't screaming all the time. I just don't understand why people have to take babies on an airplane. I mean, it's so awful, and the woman next to me kept talking and talking and the kid in back of me with his feet! Norm, and we didn't take off for hours and hours because of the smog and we had to sit around in the terminal and eat. And then the food on the plane! They're criminals. Norm, I will never set foot on another plane as long as I live. I'm a wreck. I need a cigarette. I need coffee. You don't have a cigarette on you by some chance? Either I've got to stop or you've got to start. I never can bum any from you! Please let's get a drink of something. Norm. It was just terrible. The only nice thing that happened was that this really handsome copilot talked to me for a while, but other than that, I just don't know."

What have I done? What have I done, dear God in Heaven, to deserve this? Andrea is her normal, crazy self, up on diet pills and air sickness and no sleep. I'm not so sure I'm glad to see her. Funny.

"Did you see my mother? Is she O.K.?"

"Well, I went to your house the other day — Was it yesterday or the day before? Everything's so confused in my mind, Norm. Why?"

"The time change."

"What are you talking about? The time didn't change, did it? Time can't do that, can it? I mean, it's still the same time . . . did I lose something on the plane? What happened, Norm?"

"Don't worry about it. I'll draw you a picture of it later."

"Oh! Look, there's a bar. Can we go get something to drink?"

"What do you want, some cognac?"

"No! A Coke. Oh, I want a nice big Coke with lots of ice."

"A *Coke*?"

"Yes."

"Listen, Andrea, how's my mother?"

"Oh, she's fine. She still has those bandage things

on her eyes, you know. And it's going to be all right. I mean, they did some tests in the hospital and it looks pretty good. You weren't worried, were you?"

"What happened, though? Nobody told me anything. I still wouldn't know if Richie hadn't written to me in Paris. Why did she need the operation?"

We sit down at the bar. "Will he bring us a Coke? That one over there with the white jacket. He's cute," she says, loud enough for him to hear.

"Shush," I hiss angrily at her.

"He can't understand English, can he?"

"Of course he can! This is an international airport. He's got to be able to speak English!"

Andrea looks absently around the huge modern airport. "Oh, I guess so. Well, that's good. He can get me a Coke."

"Andrea. What happened to my mother?"

"Oh, nothing. I guess she was born with something wrong with the — what's it called — the ret — the reta — "

"The retina?"

"Yeah, on both eyes. They slipped or something. And the doctors had to put them back into place. I think that what's bugging her — Oh. Would you get me a Coke, please?" She smiles her fifty-dollar-an-hour smile. He outdoes her by, I'd say, fifteen dollars and promptly returns with a Coke. "Aren't you going to have something, Norm?"

"Oh, yes. Espresso, please . . ."

"He is adorable," Andrea whispers as soon as his

back is turned. "But wait until you meet Max! He's fantastic. Really really."

"Is he in New York?"

"*No!* He's here in Milan. He's a photographer and he's arranged a whole bunch of jobs for me for two weeks. He paid for my tickets and he'll be paying me close to what I'd get in New York. But you know Daddy, even though this might be a really big break for me — I mean, you never know, I might get into a movie or something if I get into the European mags. And anyway, Daddy would *never* have let me come if you weren't here. Besides, I have a feeling that this Max is a little, you know . . ."

"That happens . . ."

"Yeah, but I couldn't tell Daddy that! But he's a nice guy and he's a really great photographer."

"Is he American?"

"No. I'm not sure what he is. Yugoslavian or Hungarian, maybe. But he speaks so many languages."

"You mean your father wouldn't have let you come alone?"

"Well, he may have, but I didn't want to go through the hassle and when he saw your telegram. Well, you know Daddy trusts you more than he does me."

"How long are you staying? Two weeks?"

"Well, it's up to you, really. As long as I'm here I might as well stay!"

(Oh, joy.)

"I brought along four hundred dollars but I don't

want to spend it because — Hey! Don't you think this Coke tastes funny?"

She shoves the glass into my face. I sip. "No."

"Tastes too sweet. They put in too much syrup." She sips another sample. "Didn't they put in too much syrup?"

"I don't know. It tastes fine to me . . ."

"How's your coffee?"

"Terrific. Listen, where's your baggage?"

She holds up what I had thought was her purse. "This is it! You know, my horoscope yesterday said not to travel. You know how Virgos hate to leave their homes. What about Pisces? Are you having any problems?"

"Yes."

"Tell me."

"Well . . . It's hard to explain and I don't think it's astrological."

"Tell me."

"Well, I keep projecting my trip and I can't get beyond Italy. I mean there's this blank when I think about Tunis and Tangier and Spain. Sicily, yes, but nothing further. All my dreams have been of bodies of water."

"Oh, well. I think I know the reason for that."

"You do?"

"I'll tell you later. It's a long story. Listen. I'm not going to finish this. Let's go."

TWENTY-EIGHT

THE TAXI is swerving into Milan.

"Fantastic. Fantastic," Andrea is saying over and over. "Fantastic! I'm really in Italy. Look at all those people. Norm. Look at them all!"

"Yeah. All Italian. What did you expect, Andrea?"

"Well, I know. But just look at them. What's there to do at night? Can we go to a nightclub or a discotheque or a bar? Where's it at, here?"

"How should I know? Have I been here before?" I'm a little tired. "Aren't you tired? You want to take a nap or something?"

"Why?"

"Because you didn't sleep last night, did you?"

"Didn't I? I think I slept. I can't sleep now, that's for sure! Look!"

"Do you want to take a bath or something?"

"Later." Andrea is still looking out the window like a dumb spaniel in a station wagon. "No. Aren't you supposed to do something in Milan? See something, I mean?"

"See?"

"Yes." She pulls out a tiny paperback book from her skirt pocket. It sort of splits open to the right page. "That's why I decided to come."

"*The Last Supper?* Not the assignment?"

"No. Who needs that? No, listen, Norm, all my life I've wanted to see *The Last Supper* up close." She points out the window. "Look at him! Look, Norm! He's adorable!" Talk about peripheral vision. She's pinching my arm.

"Cut it out, Andrea!"

"Nor-rrrmmmmmm!"

"An-dreeeea!"

She's pouting. I'm pissed.

"That's a nice dress, Norm. Where did you get it?"

"Paris."

"Paris? Really?" She's silent for a moment. "How was he?"

"Who?"

"That guy. The postcard you were writing me?"

"Oh, *that* guy. Nyeh. Not so great."

The taxi takes a sharp corner and the Duomo comes into view. "Norm! Are we far from the hotel?"

"No, we could walk it from here."

"Terrific." She raises her voice a bit. "Signore, per piacere, fermi qui."

Lo and behold, he stops. "I never knew you could speak Italian, Andrea."

"I can't," she confides, slipping me another tiny book from another pocket of her skirt. Still, it's out of character for Andrea. Not only that, but while I am multiplying and dividing dollars and lire, Andrea bounds out of the cab, hands the guy some money, and gets the change. I am out on the sidewalk staring at her in disbelief as the driver pulls out into traffic, still smiling and waving "Ciao" as he churns onward.

"Andrea," I ask, calmly. "How did you figure that out?"

"What? Figure what?"

"How much to give him?"

"Well the little meter said three thousand lire and you're supposed to give a tip and something for the second passenger so I gave him thirty-five hundred lire and I figured he would have said something if it was too little but you see he didn't." We start to walk. "You see, Norm, it's very simple. What you've got to stop doing is thinking all the time. It gets everything confused. It's like all those times you get lost on the subway. You think too much. Look, let's go in here! It's — look — it's a big old shopping center!"

We are in a vast arcade filled with people and shops and cafés. There is a high ceiling and lots of banners waving. Tables are filled with people.

We are almost through the arcade when Andrea stops in front of a café. "I'm dying for a Coke. Let's stop here."

"Andrea. I thought you wanted to see the cathedral."

"I do, but please, Norm, I'm really thirsty."

"O.K." We sit down. Almost instinctively I have the feeling that the American Express office can't be far away. "Look. I've got to go over there for a minute to pick something up." I point out the office. Andrea nods and I walk away, out of the corner of my eye catching the movement of two men over to the spot I just vacated.

When I get to the office there's a guard at the door. Just after I enter he locks the door and he only unlocks it for the few people who leave.

"May I help you?" the man behind the counter asks, checking his gold watch. His eyes dart from me to the door.

"Yes. I'd like to pick up my mail." I hand him my passport. "Cantalupo."

A faint flicker of a smile crosses his face for an instant, like a facial tic, almost, except that it stops deliberately. He goes reluctantly to the mailbox marked C. He shuffles quickly through the few envelopes and shakes his head. "I am very sorry. Nothing here." He hands back my passport.

"It's very important. Can you look again?"

He goes back to the mailbox and brings me the letters. "See for yourself."

"But I don't understand. There was supposed to be some money left for me!" Not to mention a letter from Corbett.

"It's not here." He shrugs. "I'm sorry."

"But this is urgent!"

He sighs, his deep brown eyes focusing perhaps on a plate of spaghetti on a café table across the arcade. "Signorina, I am very sorry but we are closed."

"But this is very important."

"Come back tomorrow. There is nothing I can do now; we are closed."

"But you don't seem to understand. It's got to be here. I'm out one hundred dollars!"

"Signorina. It's always urgent. It's always money being lost. It's always that I must be late for my siesta! Now, Signorina, if you don't mind, you could come back this afternoon, or you could come tomorrow morning or you could call the other offices, though I'm afraid they do not hold mail. You could go to the post office. But it will turn up. It will. They always do. There's a delay of some sort or a mail strike or the address is wrong. It will show up. But I am sorry. Right now I am late and my wife is expecting me. I am very sorry . . ."

He takes me gently by the arm and leads me to the door. He makes a little bow to the guard and we all leave, the guard's key in the door making the expulsion final.

I suppose I could start the Indignant American act, or I could ask for the name of his supervisor, but all I have the energy to do is to go back to where Andrea's sitting with her two admirers and have a nice cold drink. Oh, for a hamburger.

I suppose I should have been tipped off, the way she looked at me when I sat down at the table. I knew she knew something. And she was there, just sitting there, not saying anything. I mean, she was saying a lot but she wasn't saying what she knew I wanted to know.

"Andrea . . ."

"Oh! Norm, this is Eduardo and this is Paolo." The two men were attractive in the sort of way that men who are meticulous about their appearance always are. It's not physical at all. Maybe it's pride. "E questa Signorina é la mia amica, Norma . . ."

They were pleased. They were most fortunate. We shake hands. They drink their coffee and smile and they and Andrea communicate about the weather and about America.

"Andrea . . ." I say, after about fifteen minutes.

"Yes, Norma?"

"Andrea. Something's wrong."

"Oh, Norma, nothing's wrong. Why don't you have a drink and we'll talk about it later, O.K.?"

And so we sit in the arcade, the sun turned on outside, a slight breeze rippling through the cross-corridors, causing a second weird un-Italian, unoptimistic, un-Cantalupo shiver to run down my spine.

TWENTY-NINE

W E ARE at *The Last Supper,* Andrea and I. There
are only a few other people here, the previous occu-
pants of the empty room having been bused to their
next destination. The other buses are probably stuck
somewhere in a traffic jam. Andrea is in communica-
tion with Art, and so I try to leave her alone. It seems
strange to see her so still for such a long long time.
Something bothers me about the painting, about the
whiteness of the new side walls and the way nobody
seems to notice the other fresco on the back wall, which
is quite nice and full of life.

My problem is, I guess, that I've stared at *The Last
Supper* too long. In Catholic hospital lobbies, in holy
pictures given out for knowing the most answers in

catechism, on the shiny porcelain tiles sold in Alexander's and badly copied onto nickel Easter cards. I've also had to study it in art history class in which the slides were forty years younger than the painting in front of me, with pieces peeling. When people write about art, I don't think they ever take that into consideration. I mean, it's one thing to see a painting for a few minutes, or on the other hand to have it hanging in your house for your whole life. But to see it over and over, each time in a state worse than the time before — by the time you really get to see it, you don't care anymore and you wonder why you took that stupid bus in all this heat and bothered to come here to see it. And then, when you have to pay to see something in a church or what used to be part of a church when it should be free and open to everyone. And when you discover that the original walls were bombed out and that miraculously only these two great frescoes are left, you have to wonder — forgive me, but you do — you have to wonder if maybe the whole church wasn't bombed out and what you are seeing is not just another rotten reproduction.

I must admit that the painting itself is rather cinematic. It's like a still shot from an old silent film, everybody putting everything into the face and the gesture. I'm fascinated by Judas, cringing, his elbow almost about to push over a dish of something onto the floor.

Some little guy bounces into the room, his heels making a sharp rhythm as he walks. He stops himself in front of me for an instant and where there should have been a heel tap there's the soft explosion of his flash camera. Like a metronome, he marches out the door. The flash seems to linger longer than he. My eyes, still being on Judas, see that the face reminds me of Corbett's that night in my room in Paris.

Oh, Saint Corbett, patron saint of young American tourists, *Ora pro nobis*.

THIRTY

THE PROPRIETOR of my little Renaissance hotel is a nice guy. After all, he put in another bed for Andrea in my room. She's now lying down after having taken a long shower. I'm undressing and about to go down the hall for a shower, too.

"Do you think anyone is using the shower?" I ask, to see if she's still awake.

"Oh, no. The water isn't too hot, but I guess that's what you get in a place like this."

"Don't you like this place?"

"Yes. I suppose it's all right." She pouts and adds, "Well, it's not the Holiday Inn . . ."

"It doesn't cost twenty dollars a night, either!"

I slam the door and go down to the john. Then I go into the shower, next door. Damn middle-class American values, I say, teeth clenched. I turn on the shower. So what if it's not hot. It's water. Who does she think she is, Miss Bronx who lives in the same goddam apartment house that I do and it's not much better than this. Spoiled brat, modeling. A big-deal model. International now. Such a hotshot some photographer pays her way. Well, I can't say I'm over here on my own bread, either. Yeah, maybe Andrea does expect a whole lot more out of life than I do. Or different things, really, not more. Not the Holiday Inn! Jesus. How much bread do I have? Maybe three hundred dollars and a plane ticket and the Eurailpass and there's that credit card. Oh, I suppose it is a mistake, just like that guy said. N.A.S.A. couldn't have run out of money. Not with all the business they do. I'll keep moving right along. Maybe in Rome there's two checks.

When I get back to the room, Andrea looks like she's asleep. The room is still bright with sunlight streaming in from the courtyard. I go over to close the drapes. On a low antique bureau there is a thick wad of newspaper clippings, folded up like a kind of package. I open it up. After all, I haven't had any news from the US in nearly four weeks. The *Times*, the *Daily News*, the *Washington Post*, the *Christian Science Monitor*, *Time* magazine and *Newsweek*. I can't believe it: all the headlines contain the same initials: N.A.S.A.

One of the paper's headlines tells it all: INTERNATIONAL STUDENT SPY AGENCY: N.A.S.A., CIA AGENTS AT WORK WITHIN STUDENT TRAVEL BUSINESS.

In another there's a huge photo of a group of men,

some of whom I think I recognize. "Following Senate subcommittee meeting, subpoenas sent to N.A.S.A. director, Neil McGraw (above), and others."

The third headline reads: PART III OF SERIES ON GOVERNMENT INVESTIGATORY PRACTICES. BIG BROTHER'S LITTLE BROTHER.

One news magazine had a long article:

> Which of the estimated 12,000 students traveling abroad this summer will be spied upon courtesy of their own travel agency, N.A.S.A.? Purportedly an agency specializing in cultural exchange programs and art tours, N.A.S.A., a tax-exempt organization with spacious offices on Madison Avenue, employs about 200 young people, who, by posing as fellow students in the capitals of Europe, Asia, and the Middle East, are able to feed back information on persons involved in drug traffic, gun smuggling, and other underground activities including the I.R.A., the Black Panther party, Vietnam deserters, anarchists, and S.D.S. members. A possible relation exists between these individuals and such globally prevailing activities such as sky-jacking, bombings, and guerrilla movements.

There are pictures of several people, including a young senator.

The senator, though he could not be reached directly, issued a statement which indicates that

143

he supports cultural travel and that "The freedom of our people to travel to foreign countries
is one of the best guarantees this democracy has
of its own strength. To subject young people
to scrutiny of any sort while abroad is to under-
mine the very meaning of freedom. To make
files — no matter how confidential — on in-
dividuals is to aggravate their alienation and to
provoke contempt for our system of government."

He further indicated his own personal satis-
faction in foreign travel especially that done
during his youth . . .

I look up. Andrea is awake, watching me. Her
chestnut hair falls to one side of her oval face.

"Andrea . . ."

"Yes, Norma. I was going to tell you but I couldn't
remember all the details and I thought I'd better let you
see the articles before you got excited and started yelling."

"I never yell! Andrea! Do I yell?"

"Yes." Andrea lowers her eyes. "And I was not sure
how I should tell someone that she is probably a spy
and that she'd better be prepared for a lot of questions
when she gets home."

"Questions?"

"Well, you know, they might ask you to testify before a Senate subcommittee or something."

"Testimony!" I am yelling.

"Well, you know, all those films . . ."

"My films? You mean, after all my work? All my — Andrea, that was my one big chance. I mean, they said they were going to put my film on TV. They've no reason to lie! They did it last year and the year before. Remember those student films they had on last year? They're not a front for anyone. It's all a lie. Andrea, I can't testify. Suppose I get in trouble and land in jail?"

"You've done nothing wrong. In fact, nobody's actually done anything wrong. You don't have to worry. This is just a thing they're doing: by exposing it, you know, to get rid of it. The only thing you might have to watch out for is, you know, bad vibes and maybe a law suit."

"A law suit?"

"Yeah, *if* any of these people in your film would come to the United States and hire a lawyer and go through all that, which you can be sure they won't."

"But still . . ."

"Oh, you can get a lawyer and make some kind of written statement that you didn't know about anything, and . . ."

"But my film . . . what's going to happen to my goddam film?"

"That's up to you. That's why I thought I should come — aside from *The Last Supper* and the job — because I was afraid that if you didn't know you might be stopped at customs or if you just found out about it you might disappear or destroy your film which would look bad. If it gets subpoenaed, you'd never get to use it, anyway."

"What am I going to do?"

"Hold on. I went to see your mother, like I said, when she got out of the hospital. And she and Richie and I talked about it for a long time. Then your father came home and he said something about how every time his aunt would send him anything worth anything on the black market — jewelry, clothes, books, money — it was stolen."

"In the mail?"

"Yeah. So your mother — you know, even with those bandages she doesn't miss a thing — says, 'What Norma should do is go to Sicily, pack up the film, insure it, and mail it to a lawyer — your cousin's boy, Ned de Rosa, huh? — and then when it arrives with the customs declaration and everything, it's an empty package. Even if they don't steal it, chances are they'll open it and the light will damage it. Norma gets the insurance, the lawyer has an empty box which he can report as being broken into, and everything's taken care of for Norma. She doesn't have to be a spy, nobody knows what's in the film, she doesn't have to lie and everybody will be satisfied. If she were to destroy the film, or come back without anything, it would look very suspicious!' "

"I see. But my film will be destroyed."

"Probably. But you won't have to do it yourself."

"You mean, all those people I met — "

"Yeah," Andrea says softly, a note of envy there.

"Well," I say, "I don't have to crumble up and run home, then."

"No! Don't do that. You *mustn't* do that!"

"Why not?"

"Because, like I said, I was talking to your parents and I got the feeling that they, well, they felt bad for you. They kept saying how hurt you were going to be. And your father was mad, because . . ."

"Because somebody made his little baby cry. I know. That's Dad, all right."

"Your mother, though, you know she's had a lot of time lately to think about things, 'cause she's had to keep so still."

"What about her coffee klatch?"

"Oh, they don't start dropping over until about eleven o'clock and they don't stay long, she says."

"Good old Mrs. Levy. And Mrs. Pinto and Miss Whalen. How does she have any time to think?"

"She does. And she said that now that she knows how close she came to blindness, she says — at least she tells me — that she really understands what you were talking about" — Andrea pauses for a long look at me — "but she didn't explain."

I smile. "Oh, that. I'm pretty sure I know what she meant."

"Do you think this business is going to work out?"

"Yeah. It does. It always does," I say, picking up my hairbrush. "It has to."

THIRTY-ONE

I MEAN, you probably think I'm crazy. Yeah, I can tell you do. I mean, I'm not so dumb that I can't see that. You're saying to yourself that this chick is not for real. That these things don't really happen to people. Not to you, anyway. Well, don't be so sure. I mean, like you probably expect to hear how when I got back to New York I got a dozen red roses wired to me from Corbett. I didn't. I may never hear from him again, except that my mother *did* get a call from someone but she forgot to write down his name and he said he'd call back but he didn't so maybe it was Corbett. Maybe it wasn't. But like I said, I haven't heard from him. And Joe. You expect that maybe he and I are getting married. No. He's still going to night school and he's engaged to Andrea.

And you probably think I should tell you all about what happened on the rest of the trip, but you can guess. Andrea kept on drinking Cokes and hating the cheap hotels we stayed in and we talked Max into taking all his photographs in Sicily so that we could mail my film off from there. And we did mail it to that lawyer in New York and it did get stolen. That's really about all you have to know.

But I suppose I should let you know that we had a lot of fun. Andrea even got on the cover of *Gioia* and a couple of other magazines. We bought a lot of clothes and didn't have very much money left to get back with. I almost sold my camera, but then I decided that wasn't very smart and that I could make a lot more films, and that even if this whole thing went down the drain, I learned a lot technically and I think I know what I'm going to make my next film about for my Cinema IV class next quarter. Andrea is going to help. Richie too.

And with the leftover film we did shoot some nice scenes in Sicily — my father's relatives, the house my grandparents lived in when they were first married, of the beach down the hill, and of the water and the soft sand and the buildings which seemed pale in the intense sun, and the vegetable and fruit and bread and fish men and the egg lady and the kids selling melons and the songs they sang while they walked past the kitchen windows, and of an old aunt of Dad's stirring a pot of soup while the littlest little boy you could imagine shook his blond curls of the salt water that was still left after his run up the hill from the beach. And of Max and some of our cousins and friends waving us good-bye and hugging us, and of us crying a bit, and of Andrea dragging her heels as we boarded the jet on the return flight and all the trains we had to take in between.

And you probably want to know about what I said to the Senate subcommittee, but I didn't say anything because the testimony of other people made while we were away was sufficient and all the publicity had died down by the time we got home, and all I had to do was make a written statement.

Oh, and my mother's eyes are better than they were before, though not perfect, and they're talking about going to Europe someday. Maybe next summer. My mother likes the leather purse I bought her in Palermo, so much she's saving it for things like Thanksgiving and Christmas and birthdays. (Birthdays are a big thing with her.)

And you probably think maybe I'm bitter about the whole thing and about Corbett and about not having my career launched with the film. Well, it bothers me. All of it. But I'm glad it happened. I had a lot of fun, even the part where, on our very last day, Andrea and I had so little money we were eating fried potatoes out of those vending machines in Amsterdam and stealing little packs of ketchup for dessert. And I suppose you could say there's a lesson in all of this. But I haven't found it. I mean art or music or films, they make sense. But life? It just keeps going on until it stops and there's nothing you can do about it except be glad you've got it, even though you're not quite sure it's doing you any good. It's like earwax, you know? No matter how hard you think about it, there's not much you can do with it.